TURMOIL & OTHER STORIES

TURMOIL

& Other Stories

A collection of short stories

by

WAYNE F. BURKE

Adelaide Books
New York / Lisbon
2020

TURMOIL & OTHER STORIES
A collection of short stories
By Wayne F. Burke

Copyright © by Wayne F. Burke
Cover design © 2020 Adelaide Books

Published by Adelaide Books, New York / Lisbon
adelaidebooks.org

Editor-in-Chief
Stevan V. Nikolic

For any information, please address Adelaide Books
at info@adelaidebooks.org

or write to:
Adelaide Books
244 Fifth Ave. Suite D27
New York, NY, 10001

ISBN: 978-1-953510-86-0

Printed in the United States of America

pour mon grandmere, Rosa Trahan Burke

Contents

I Remember Buddy

THE engine of the 1964 Buick Electra hums like a big cat. Streetlights flicker across the hood, over the windshield. The black highway is slick from an overnight rain. The dark sky glows above the lime kiln, behind the grammar school that sits like a fortress on the hill.

"You sit in the back," Uncle Albert says, driving one-handed, ember tip of his Pall Mall cigarette bright red.

Cigarette smoke mingles with the smell of leather seats and Albert's after-shave lotion. The lime kiln emits a shriek; the barn-like buildings are huddled shoulder to shoulder in a stewing cloud of white dust.

The driver's side window hisses down. Albert snuffs his cigarette out through the gap. Houses and brick tenements lining Friend Street sit silent, dark.

"Hope they get the game in," Albert says, shifting his weight, the seat springs groaning. "Say it's going to clear, but they're wrong half the time..." Albert swings the car into a side street, stops before a thin peak-roofed two-story house. A lighted window on the first floor turns black.

I climb over the front seat-back, drop onto the clear plastic of the rear seat cover. The car door opens, lighting the interior. Buddy eases himself into the front seat.

"Ga'morning."

Buddy's head swings my way. "Who is that, Al? Butch?"

"No, that is the other one. Eddie."

The car door slams shut.

"You remember Buddy, don't you?" Albert calls. He wheels the car back onto the hill. Across the valley, the sky is smoky-gray above the rim of the sloping mountain range.

Buddy uncaps a large thermos and pours some of its contents into a cup. "Heard the weather report," he says. "Going to clear," he states, like a fact of life.

The liquid smells like coffee mixed with medicine.

"I talked to Walt," Albert says. "Dale can give us three minutes—in an' out."

"Great. Walt going to meet us there? Take us in?" Buddy passes the steaming cup to Albert.

"Yeah. He says so. Gate 19."

Albert steers the car south, out of town. The droning engine is soothing—like the rhythmic wash of a waterfall.

The car engine purrs like an over-excited cat. The straight city street is enclosed like a tunnel by two contiguous walls of buildings. The buildings gray like the sky.

Uncle Albert stares straight ahead. A roll of fat shaped like a knockworst bulges over the collar of his white shirt worn beneath a silky dark blue suit coat.

The car speeds past block after block.

The radio plays "Under the Boardwalk" by The Drifters.

Endless-seeming rows of buildings line the street. Flocks of people on the sidewalks. Negroes; every one, a Negro.

"Where are we?" I have seen Negroes, but not many, and never congregated.

"Harlem," Albert states.

The car slows, comes to a swift sudden halt. A parade of Negroes marches past. At the end of the parade a huge man, wearing a black overcoat, straw boater with red band; his shovel-sized face in a scowl.

"Sonny Liston," I say, pointing.

Albert bats my hand down. "No, it isn't," he says softly, as if not wanting to be over-heard.

The car merges with a stream of traffic flowing like water from a faucet.

"Can you believe Big Mouth beating Liston?" Albert asks.

"If that fight wasn't fixed, I'm a monkey's uncle," Buddy says.

The Buick floats in the stream of traffic like a chip carried on the current of a river.

"Patterson will shut his mouth," Albert says.

"You think so?" Buddy rests a paw on the seat-back.

"I know so."

Buildings stacked like toy blocks and towers of stone high in the sky chock-full of coal-black clouds. Buddy takes a gulp from his thermos, passes the cylinder to Albert. Raindrops splatter the windshield. The windshield wipers keep tempo to "Baby Love" sung by the Supremes.

YANKEE STADIUM, a sign reads. 1 MILE.

The tails of Albert's suit coat flare over the humps of his broad hips. His short legs move quickly and his polished black leather shoes scuff the damp cement walkway. Beside him, Buddy strides jerkily with his thick dwarfish legs; his hands in jacket pockets and a newly-bought NY YANKEES cap like an overturned bowl on his over-sized head.

The stadium is high above, high as a tall building. People passing and in the crowd carry NY YANKEE pennants and wear NY YANKEE caps and the NY YANKEE logo on NY YANKEE-colored clothing. Smell of pop corn, peanuts, hot dogs, cigars...Car horns from the city bleat in the distance: tires squeal, sirens wail...

Albert wobbles to a halt. "Catch my breath," he huffs, leaning against a stadium column. Buddy gawks at two women: one wearing bat-wing-shaped glasses and a beehive hairdo; one a Beatles style cut and earrings resembling tiny baseballs. The beehive hairdo wears knee-high black go-go dancer boots. Albert straightens, lips curled in a wrought smile. The women quicken their pace. Albert hitches his pants up over an inner tube-shaped roll of fat. He stares at me, expression quizzical. "I hope you know how lucky you are," he says. "Nobody ever took me to Yankee Stadium when I was your age." The dark brown eyes stare like I am the cause of his not going to Yankee Stadium.

"After one, Al," Buddy says.

I jog behind the door-width of Albert's back to keep up.

GATE 19. PRIVATE. KEEP OUT.

"Hey Walt! WALT!" Buddy wades into the crowd, a phalanx before the gate.

Tall gangling long-armed Walt, leaning against the chain-link fence, springs forward. "About time!" he shouts. "I was ready to give up on you birds!" Walt grins; his greased hair is combed into a pompadour; a racing form is jammed into his pants pocket; he flicks his cigarette to the pavement. Fingers the elastic stretch-band waist of his satiny NY YANKEES jacket. "Hello, Squirt," he says.

"Hi."

He musses my hair (which I do not like). "You ready? Let's go!" Walt commands. "We are late!"

Walt pushes through the phalanx to a door; calls to a face behind the steel mesh screen of the door's window; slips a square of paper through a slit cut into the mesh. Buddy elbows aside a pimple-faced teenager. Albert clenches my jacket collar, yanks me through the opened door into a long low ceiling-ed gray corridor. A uniformed guard walks beside Walt. It is quiet as church in the corridor.

"Mind your manners," Albert growls in my ear, hand still clenching. "Don't speak unless spoken to, you hear?"

A door in the wall is covered by a shiny NY YANKEE emblem big as a hula hoop. The door opens: a Yankee-blue carpeted anteroom is walled by steel mesh screens. A bald dark-eyed man wearing a NY YANKEE warm-up jacket stares from behind the anteroom door. Behind the man a wall painted in the pin-stripe pattern of the Yankee uniform.

"Hey, Long!" the man calls, "your frens is heer!"

Dale Long, taller than Walt, peers down through the mesh. The dark-eyed man unbolts the door.

"Hello Dale!" Walt says. "How you hittin' 'em?"

"So-so," Dale Long says, extending a hand which Walt, Albert, and Buddy shake in turn. "How are you guys doing?"

Long wears rubber shower sandals and half his uniform. His white pin-striped pants look soft as velvet. His red-tinged face is lined but his body, beneath a white Yankee's t-shirt, is stringently muscled as a greyhound. "Come'on," he says, "I want you to meet someone."

The locker room, wide and long as a basketball court, is carpeted by a Yankee-blue carpet, orange-colored lockers the size of closets line the pin-striped walls, orange-colored chairs before the lockers. Smell of shoe leather, Ben Gay, talcum powder, and sweat. The Yankee logo on floor and ceiling. Ball players—I read the names, TRESH, BERRA, KUBEK—dress at their lockers. Other players, men, move about. From a radio, Roy Orbison sings "Sweet Dreaming Baby."

Long approaches a thick-necked, broad-backed player, half a foot shorter, who is bent lacing a cleat. "Hey Mick," Long says, "say hello to some guys I use to play ball with in high school."

Mick turns. Long clasps Albert and Walt by their shoulders.

"How yawl doin'?" Mick drawls. "Was he any good," he asks, motioning to Long while shaking Albert's hand.

"Not ba-ba-ba-bad," Albert says.

Mick laughs, white teeth square like Chicklets in his square face and jaw, and chin with a cleft in the middle. He holds his hand out to Walt.

"It is an honor to meet you, Micky." Walt begins a curtsy, stops himself halfway.

"Thank you," Mick says. He extends a hairy ham-shaped forearm to Buddy.

Buddy pumps Mick's hand, staring, transfixed.

Mick cracks a grin, pulls away from Buddy, reaches, pats my head. "You play ball, son?"

I nod.

"He's in the Little League," Albert says.

Mick's crew cut blonde hair and square face are wreathed by a halo of golden light. His eyes blue as swimming pool water.

"Any good?" he asks, eyes twinkling.

I shrug; I am good but to say so is immodest.

"He's shy," Albert says, placing a hand on my shoulder.

"Going to play for the Yankees?" Mick continues.

"Umm..." I am going to play for the Red Sox but do not want to hurt Mick's feelings by saying so.

Mick turns to his locker. I duck Albert's hand. Mantle turns back, holds a snow-white baseball out to me.

"Thanks!" I pluck the ball from the sausage-shaped fingers.

Mick pulls his jersey on over boulder-like shoulders. "You boys have one on me," he says. Buddy cackles, throws a parting wave. Long steers Albert and Walt toward the anteroom. Buddy glances around, reaches, plucks a jersey from a chair back, and stuffs the shirt inside his jacket.

"Is it true about Terry's arm," Walt whispers to Long.

"I can't tell you that," Long says.

The dark-eyed man scurries forward, keys jangling like chimes at his waist.

"Just nod," Walt whispers, "yes or no."

"So long," Dale Long calls, "don't do anything I would not do!"

"Sure Dale," Albert says, "and what would that be?"

Long giggles.

The guard escorts us to the door.

Back out in the corridor, Walt turns to Albert: "that son of a bitch," he says.

I hear thunder.

I wake in the dark, in the car, the soft shush of car tires rolling over a rain-soaked road. Albert motionless as a statue before the wheel, a blank bored stupefied look on his face. The windshield wipers beat steadily, moving furiously in tandem like two indomitable soldiers fighting an army.

I look out at familiar houses—dark forms in the mist. Rain drops beat on the roof like a rapping of knuckles.

Albert turns the car into our street, the corner streetlight shining like a beacon above the squat mailbox.

I feel the baseball in my pocket.

The gravel of our driveway pops beneath the car tires. The car slides to a halt before the back porch. "Tell your grand-mother not to wait up for me," Albert says.

I open the door, step out into a cold rain. The porch light illuminates silver threads of falling rain drops.

"Don't slam the door!" Albert barks.

I swing the door shut. The car takes off like it knows where it is going.

The Boxing Champ

Chooch Rondini, a sixth grader, walks up to me and says I have to fight Pete Larson.

I lean back against the rough brick of the schoolhouse.

"Why do I have to fight?" I ask.

Chooch looks hurt by my question. He cannot believe what he is hearing, he says; cannot believe I would back down from a fight. My brother Mitch would be ashamed of me Chooch says and so would the rest of my family, even Anne, my sister in the fourth grade; she'd be ashamed of me, too.

Mitch runs across the gravel drive, feet crunching stones, high top black sneakers kicking up clouds of dust. He skids to a halt beside me.

"The kid is yellow," olive-skinned Chooch tells Mitch. "No guts—he won't do it."

Mitch towers over me. His goggled eyes stare down at me from behind the panes of his black-rimmed glasses. He looks like a crew-cut Clark Kent.

"I thought you said your brother had guts," Chooch complains. "Ain't that what you said?"

Mitch asks if I want to play baseball with the neighborhood team during the summer. I say I do. "Well, this is your training," he says, "and if you don't train you can't play baseball."

"Exactly!" Chooch shouts. "You don't fight, you don't play." Chooch looks grave; he shakes his peanut-shaped head. "I kid you not," he adds.

I say, "alright."

Chooch claps me on the back. "I knew you had guts," he crows.

I follow Chooch and Mitch around the school building. I feel good. I feel like I belong.

A circle of kids has formed in the yard. Husky, pasty-faced Skin Canoli, another sixth grader, holds skinny cue-ball headed Pete Larson in the center of the circle. Chooch kneels beside me and show me how he wants me to punch: "pow pow pow," he says, shooting out a left jab.

I mimic his motions. He tells me to show him a right-cross. He pats my head, tells Mitch that with the right amount of training I could become another Floyd Patterson. Skin whistles, a piercing screech that momentarily eclipses the murmuring drone of the lime kiln next door to the school. Mitch pushes me out toward Pete who stands like a statue, arms at his sides. Kids scream for Pete and me to kill each other. Pete runs but is shoved back into the circle. I jab: pow pow pow. Pete turns and flees, worms his way through the wall of kids and runs across the green lawn. A handful of kids run after him yelling that Pete is "chicken." Pete escapes around the corner of the Bellini's house.

"TKO!" Skin announces, holding my arm up above my head.

Kids pat me on the back. I hear swarthy-skinned, pompadoured Jerry Boa tell freckle-faced Garibaldi that I am tough. I wonder if Jerry is right.

After the fight, I fight all the time, every day. Chooch my trainer, Mitch my coach. I fight almost all the boys in my class, and after beating most everyone, I fight kids from other classes. I always win. Soon, everyone in the school knows about me being a champ, and kids I do not even know act like they want to be my friend. Also, according to Jerry Boa, who sits behind me in class, cute black-haired Ramona Brown, a third-grader, has said she likes me.

I do not know what to think about girls liking me. I tell Chooch what Ramona has said. He acts upset, and tells me to stay away from girls.

"Girls are no good," he says. "They are nothing but trouble. You start messing with girls and you're 'kaput.' I kid you not."

After my Uncle Albert hears about me being a boxing champ, he says he wants to see my stuff. After lunch one day, he tells me to follow him out to the backyard. In the shade of a backyard tree, Albert kneels on the soft green grass and tells me to hit him.

Albert wears his pine tree-green gas station uniform; he smells like gasoline and sweat. His pie-shaped face is dark, smudged with grease. "Hit me," he demands.

I throw a few punches at the shopping-bag-sized head. He blocks the punches, his hands tough as leather, rough as bark. He giggles. His front teeth like yellow P.E.D.S. "Come'on, you're so tough," he urges.

I throw an uppercut. The punch lands on Albert's chest, above his heart, beneath the white oval–'AL' written in red in the oval—on his shirt.

Albert's face darkens like a storm cloud; he reaches and slaps me across the face.

I bawl.

19

"Hah, just as I figured," Albert smirks, hauling himself to his feet. "Nothing but a little girl, that's all. A sissy."

The screen door of the house swings open and slaps shut. Gramp stands on the back porch, his arms akimbo.

"He hit me," I blubber, pointing at Albert, who is a little over five feet and a little under three hundred pounds.

"I didn't touch him," Albert vociferously states.

"You leave the boy alone!" Gramp shouts, snarling, his bald head shining in the sun. "I don't want you touching him!"

Albert shakes a cigarette from his pack of Pall Malls. "He cries over nothing—a little tap, that's all." He lights his cigarette from a silver lighter he snaps open with a flick of his wrist. He stares at me, eyes narrowed to slits within the cloud of sooty smoke wreathing his head.

Gramp turns and strides back into the house, muttering about Albert keeping his hands to himself.

Albert, smoking like a chimney, waddles to his car parked in the drive.

I train in the cellar. I punch a padded sideboard and jump rope (my sister's rope) while playing the new Chubby Checker song "The Twist" on the record player. "Let's twist again like we did last summer," Chubby sings, "let's twist again like we did last year."

Having won all my fights, I guess that Chooch and the others, like Jerry Boa, are right. I really am tough. I am going to be another Floyd Patterson.

In my next fight I face Stevie Sondrini, a chubby, white-skinned, four-eyed marshmallow. Unlike my first fight, I can't wait to get started. I am hungry for more victories, eager to extend my popularity. I have no doubt Stevie will be my next victim. At Skin's whistle I rush in to finish Stevie off quickly.

He punches me. His fist feels like the blunt end of a stick on my face. My feet walk away from me like disobedient puppies. My knees buckle like loose hinges; I land on my back. The stones of the schoolyard make an uncomfortable bed. Chooch peers down at me; his face swims in the blue sky. A white cloud halo's his head.

"You all right?" he asks with an odd smile I do not like the look of.

Course I am all right: I am tough: I am the champ, the next Floyd Patterson! I get up and approach Sondrini. I tell myself to fight smart, not rush in. Kids scream for Sondini and me to kill each other. I jab and circle to my right. I realize that I hate Sondrini. Hate his guts. I want to pound his face to a bloody pulp. I want to kill him. I rush in.

He watches me, his round, pale blue eyes open wide and unafraid; his clenched fists held beneath his chubby chin. He ducks my right hand, bobs up beside me, and punches me in the face...I hit the stones, face-down. Someone shouts that Sondrini is the new champ. I am too hurt to care. The voices move away, growing fainter. I roll over, in the dirt, feeling as alone as the first invertebrate to crawl from the sea onto land must have felt. Mitch, Chooch, Skin, all my "friends," where are they? I sit up; my eye is swollen almost shut, chunks of gravel are stuck in my face, and a half-dollar-sized hole is ripped from the knee of my new pants. I am concerned about the hole.

I return home after school. My grandmother looks up from the kitchen table when the door slaps shut.

"Bon Dieu! Nom d'une pipe!" she shouts. "Look what you have done to your pants!"

She springs out of her chair, waving her arms. "I can't sew a hole like that!" her teacup rattles around in its saucer.

She shoves her chair back across the tiled floor. The chair legs screech.

"What did you do?" she demands. "Throw yourself on the ground?"

"I fell! It was not my fault!"

"Was not your fault! Whose fault was it, I'd like to know! I suppose it was my fault!" She looks at the hole, head bent, snow white hair collapsed beneath the dark threaded hair net.

"Take them off," she barks.

She turns and marches, arms swinging, toward the dining room. "More work!" she shouts. "Work work work, that is all I do around this damn house!"

She sits and test pumps the foot lever of her sewing machine. The machine makes a whirring sound, like a whip whistling through air. I stand behind her, holding my pants.

"Je m'en fiche! Laisser les aller-nu-fesse!" She stabs a finger inside a drawer of the machine. "I am no better than a maid in this house," she crabs. "No, I am worse off than a maid, a maid gets paid! What do I get? Nothing! A kick in the rear end!"

She glances back at me. "Put those down," she orders, "and go! Leave me alone! Lassez-moi seule!"

I tell everyone at school that Sondrini had a rock in his hand when he hit me. It sounds plausible—could even be true. No one believes me, I can tell; but I keep repeating the story until Chooch tells me "cool the jaws." I was beat fair and square Chooch says. And it is my own fault I got beat. He told me not to fool around with girls, but I did not listen to him.

"I told you they'd get you in trouble, didn't I?" Chooch rubs a hand over his close-shaven head like a man with many worries.

I tell him I had only done it twice. Once when I chased Ramona across the school yard and another time I played house with her and she kissed me. But I did not really want her to, and when she tried again I said 'no,' because I was in training and could not let her do it anymore.

Chooch looks sad. He says he will have to talk to Mitch and they will decide whether or not to keep training me. He says that in the meantime, I better stay away from girls because if he or Mitch catches me fooling with them, I will be dropped like a hot potato.

"I kid you not," he adds.

On Saturday afternoon I sit at my grandfather's bar alongside my new best friend, Jerry Boa. Jerry stares, bug-eyed, down the length of the long polished bar. He is impressed. I eat a piece of cheese popcorn and drink Coca-Cola from a glass. It is sunny outside but dark in the bar. The black and white television, high in the bar corner, gives off a brilliant light. Jerry and I watch "I Love Lucy." Ethel's husband Fred looks like Gramp, only Fred is thinner.

Gramp stands behind the bar; he is square-shouldered, egg-shaped, sharp-eyed and hawk-nosed. He wears a white apron over a white, button-down shirt. A cigarette burns between his fingers. The smoke floats above his head, below a picture of Franklin D. Roosevelt hung above the cash register.

After Grandma hears about me being in the bar she says I am not to go there anymore as "it is no place for children."

I tell Grandma she is "dumb." We are in the kitchen; the moon-faced wall clock tick-tocks. Grandma bristles, her eyes flash beneath the lenses of her black, bat-wing-shaped glasses.

"Don't call me dumb," she shouts. "Tu es stupide!" She prods me toward the corner of the kitchen with the tips of her work-hardened fingers.

"Kneel down," she commands.

I kneel, convinced of the truth of my statement. My knees press against the tiles, white squares sparsely streaked with dull colors. The floor thrusts itself back up at me. I sit back on the calves of my legs.

"On your knees! Stay there half-an-hour. Learn some respect!"

The wooden legs of Grandma's ironing board creak and groan. The sweet smell of steam-ironed clothes fills the kitchen. The floor thrusts itself like fists into my knees. The long horses' legs of the ironing board stamp the floor, protesting against the hot iron.

"Turn around! Kneel!"

The half-hour stretches before me like an eternity. I know I will not make it. I wonder if I really am tough.

Dog Days

1.

The devil living inside Sterl's stomach told Sterl to put rocks and dirt in the gas tank of his brother Joe's car. "I told the devil 'no,'" Sterl explained, looking down at a crack in the sidewalk that wound beneath his brown work boots like a river on a map. "But the devil said 'do it.' I shouldn't have listened to him. Now Joe's mad...Real mad."

Fourteen year old Jackie Garibaldi smiled. "Well, tell Joe you're sorry," Jackie enthused. "Tell Joe it was the devil who did it." Jackie patted his flattop haircut; he sculpted the bed of nails with his fingers.

"I did," Sterl said, focusing moist puppy dog's eyes. "I told him! He wouldn't believe me. Joe thinks I lie." Sterl's pitted pock-marked face flushed red. "Joe says he will call the cops on me. I don't like cops. No, I don't." Sterl shook his head, as if in answer to a question. His jet-black pompadour swayed with the motion. He plunged his hands into front pockets of his shiny green work pants. "Tell me, Mike," he said to four-foot tall, spike-haired and snot-nosed Walter O'Ryan: "tell me how to make the devil shut up."

Walter, wearing a torn and dirty white t-shirt and urine-stained pants—the dried urine leaving a topographical map-like pattern of concentric ovals formed by the salt crust lines spreading from his crotch outward—blushed, and a peal of involuntary laughter brightened his habitually sullen expression. "I don't know," he said, like a complaint.

Sterl's dog-face swung over the heads of the semi-circle of kids, muscles topping his square-shouldered build stretching the fabric of his green work shirt, made of the same satiny material as his pants. "What should I do, Mike?" he asked Jackie. "Tell me, Mike—how can I make the devil leave me alone?"

Jackie's eyes narrowed. He cracked his knuckles and flexed his arms. Egg-shaped biceps bulged beneath his white t-shirt. "Just tell the devil, 'no!'"

"He won't listen to me," Sterl complained. "He hurts me, Mike. The devil hurts me. Hurts me bad—in here–" Sterl pointed to the middle of his stomach. "The devil stabs me here, Mike!"

Twelve-year-old Weed Garibaldi, husky, dough-faced, crew-cut, stared at Sterl's stomach. Beside Weed, astride a bicycle, anemic-looking Skully Larson, a hatchet-faced pubescent bean-pole, snickered.

"It's not funny!" Sterl barked.

Skully's complexion turned from vanilla to titanium white.

"He hurts me! He does! The devil hurts me inside!"

"I'll tell you what, Sterl," Jackie said. "Eat oranges. Eat oranges everyday! A bag of oranges!"

"You think so, Mike? Think that will help me? Do you? Will that shut the devil up?" Sterl spoke with mounting excitement. "Will it? Will it, Mike? You think so?"

Spike O'Ryan, three-foot-tall with a round hydrocephalic head, and Edwardo "Eddie" Decensi, swarthy, slightly taller than Spike, and dressed in a Little Lord Fauntleroy outfit of brown loafers, blue shorts and matching jacket, white button-down shirt and red bow tie, nodded affirmatively.

"I know so," Jackie said, snapping his fingers and displaying sharp incisors in a smile of white teeth.

"I'll try it," Sterl said. "I'll go to the store. Joe lets me charge at the store. The store likes me. I'll do it, Mike! Right now!"

Sterl turned and stalked away like a happy Frankenstein. "Thanks, Mike" he called over his shoulder. "Thanks a lot!"

2.

Sterl plodded up the sunny street, sweat drops the size of grapes covering his face. His shirt sleeves rolled to his elbows and a plastic bag of oranges cradled in his arm like a baby. He bit down on an orange. "Ow!" he cried, face reddening. "Cut it out!" he declaimed, halting mid-plod. "I mean it!" Orange juice showered his shirt and boots. "Stop it! Stop it, damn you!"

From the front doorway of a mustard-colored two-story house, Mr. Larson, looking out his screen door window, hooted. "Sterling is mad at something," he commented.

Flaccid-bodied Mrs. Larson, stepping from her kitchen to the doorway, glanced to the street.

"Damn you! I'll kill you!" Sterl shouted.

Distaste altered Mrs. Larson's mild features.

Sterl stared hostilely at a beagle ambling across the street. The dog eyed Sterl with intelligent scrutiny as it waddled to the sidewalk.

Sterl spit orange rind into the gutter. Juice ran down his chin. "Hey, Mike!" he called. "Hey! Mike!"

Jackie Garibaldi stood in a black-topped driveway beside the two-story slate-roofed Garibaldi residence. A green and yellow striped garter snake, held in Jackie's hands, flicked its tongue in Sterl's direction, tasting air fragrant with vegetable smells of the Garibaldi's backyard garden.

Weed and Skully sat on the stoop of the back porch.

Walter O'Ryan, emerging from beneath the front porch of the sway-backed ramshackle O'Ryan residence next door, called—in a parody of friendliness: "hi Sterl!" Walter walked toward the road; he motioned to the bag of oranges. "Can I have one?"

Sterl stared. "No, you can't. I need them. For my stomach."

"Just one!" Walter whined.

"No."

Walter's smile congealed in a resentful pout. Jackie, Weed, and Skully, came within hailing distance of Sterl. Jackie's new KED sneakers shone bright as light bulbs against the black driveway.

"My stomach, Mike," Sterl intoned, "still hurts me. How come, Mike?"

"Why are you eating oranges?" Jackie demanded.

The bag hung from Sterl's hand like an over-sized dumb-bell. "Because. Because you said to, Mike."

"I didn't say 'oranges'! I said 'doughnuts'! Eat doughnuts!" Jackie winked at Weed.

"That's right! He said 'doughnuts'," Weed offered.

Skully nodded agreeably, hands in front pockets of his clam diggers.

Sterl glanced critically at the oranges. "You did?"

"He did," Walter, looking to Jackie, enthused. "He said..." 'doughnuts.'"

Sterl stared at Walter. Walter stared at the oranges. Jackie draped the snake around his neck like a tie. The snake's thimble-sized head swimmingly wavered across Jackie's chest.

"Here," Sterl said, swinging the bag of oranges to Walter.

Walter caught the bag like a football against his chest. His eyes widened. A yellow smile of broken teeth. "Gee! Thanks, Sterl!"

Sterl turned and plodded down the street.

3.

A mailman wearing a white safari helmet side-stepped a dried dog turd lying on the sidewalk as he looked up at Sterl, advancing, a box of doughnuts under his arm, his mouth rimmed with white powdered sugar, and a long white beard of the powder down his shirt front.

"How is it going, Sterl?" the mailman asked.

"It hurts, it hurts..." Sterl gloomily chanted.

The mailman stepped aside. Sterl pinched a doughnut from the box and raised it to his lips. White powder rained down onto his shirt. He slowed at the entrance to a driveway, staring at a middle-aged gray haired dome-headed man running water from a hose over the hood of a car. Droplets of water, dripping onto the asphalt, sparkled like diamonds in the morning sunshine. "Hello Dolly," the man sang, "you're looking swell DOLLY..."

"It hurts, Mike!" Sterl shouted. "Mike! It hurts! It hurts, Mike!"

The man glanced to the street; the ridges of his brow, beneath the dome, furrowed; he focused on the shimmering hood and dollops of splashing water...

Sterl halted in the shade of a horse chestnut tree overhanging the street. He stared at the gingerbread facade of a house across the road. The face-like facade stared back. A gleaming tan and silver Buick Electra floated up the street, past Sterl, who stared, face craggily frozen in mid-chew. "It hurts!" he called to the fat man driving the car. The fat man scowled. A cloud of dust and exhaust fumes wafted over Sterl like a desert breeze.

4.

Sterl tread through a cow pasture, stepping mawkishly around the cow flops. The sun seared Sterl's head; burnt grass and bleached straw crackled beneath his boots. He heard shouts of the ball players in the ball-field adjacent the pasture.

At pasture's edge, Sterl bent and clutched his gut. The ballplayers cheered. "Stop it," Sterl barked, "cut it out!" He stepped from the pasture onto the manicured grass of the ball-field. Red face out-thrust, he walked down the chalked right field line. "Mike!" he hollered, "it is not working, Mike! My stomach, Mike! It still hurts! It hurts worse, Mike!"

"Go'wan home, Sterl," cue-ball headed dark-eyed Chief Gamarsh hollered from his third base position.

Sterl focused a troubled gaze on Jackie Garibaldi, sitting beside Weed, Spike, and Skully, on a gnawed and gouged wooden bench along the first-base line.

"The devil still hurts me, Mike," Sterl said, rubbing his belly. "Hurts me bad...You told me wrong, Mike. You said the devil wouldn't bother me no more. You were wrong! You were wrong, Mike!"

Jackie, looking past Sterl, adjusted his ball cap.

Barrel-shaped, cherubim-faced Tank Sherman, ran down the first base line, his stumpy legs churning, sneaker's kicking up puffs of dust...

Jackie stood and strode to the on-deck circle.

"I thought you were my friend, Mike," Sterl said, following Jackie.

Jackie flexed a ball-bat in his hands. "I am your friend, Sterl," he scolded.

"No, you're not my friend. No, you're not, Mike. You're not my friend!" Sterl's face flushed crimson. "Stop it, damn you!" he screamed. "I'LL KILL YOU!"

Jackie leapt back, eyes widened in surprise.

Sterl stepped toward Jackie, clumsily, like a man trying to find his way in the dark.

Jackie brandished the ball-bat. "Go'wan!" he hissed, back-peddling.

Sterl lumbered like a drunken bear. "Stop it! Damn you! I'll kill you! I mean it!"

Players, converging from the field and benches, circled Sterl like a tribe of pygmies. Weed, Spike, Skully, Tank, screamed in unison; Chief waved the other available ball-bat about Sterl's head; Sterl lurched as if propelled from behind, hands upheld as if to ward off a blow. The circle closed, expanded elastically. Baseball gloves buffeted Sterl's head and shoulders.

Jackie dug his foot into the infield dirt, his lips compressed, finger's whitening on the shaft of the poised and wavering bat. Sterl lumbered forward. The head of the bat moved in an arc and knocked against Sterl's skull...Sterl fell onto the grass, rolled over onto his back; his puppy dog's eyes staring up at the blue sky...

"Damn devil," he said.

A Beautiful Day in the Neighborhood

The diner sparkled with silver gleamings, glass surfaces shining, sunlight slanting through the side windows and door. Eddie Kelly felt the dime in the pocket of his Bermuda shorts. Wafer-thin and rougher on one side. A vertical column of pies, cherry, apple, banana cream, sat in a glass case on the counter top. A radio behind the counter played "Ode to Billy Joe." Beside Eddie, a fat truck driver sat perched on one of the red leather-topped stools. Smoke from the driver's cigarette swirled; he held a newspaper in front of his face.

TIGERS BEAT SOX, Eddie read.

A big semi-trailer truck roared into the yard and stopped before the EILEEN's DAIRY BAR sign at the edge of the highway. Air brakes hissed like an exhaled breath.

"Hi Eddie," Alma, the waitress, said. "What can I get you?"

"Ice cream," Eddie said. "Butter pecan." Alma bent to the silver cooler behind the counter. She reached deep into the cooler, her white waitress-dress tightening around her bottom.

Eddie looked away.

23 DEAD IN NEWARK RIOT

Alma straightened. A tall flat-chested girl; hair in a bun, plain unmarked face white like her long slender arms and legs. She molded a fist of ice cream, on a silver-gray scoop, to a sugar cone.

Eddie remembered the night in winter when Johnny Garibaldi asked what he, Eddie, thought of Alma, and Eddie had said, without thinking, "a rose yet to bloom," the words coming unbidden to his lips.

Johnny had clapped his hands delightedly. He had marched, wobbly-legged on black figure skates, from the warm dimly lit skating rink hut. And had told everyone on the rink what Eddie had said. For long afterward, whenever Alma's name was mentioned, someone was sure to say, "a rose yet to bloom."

Over the course of two seasons, the phrase had been forgotten, Eddie reflected. Or had it? He hoped so. It had caused him a humiliating amount of embarrassment...

"Thanks," he said, reaching for the cone. He set the dime in Alma's thin slender hand.

"Thank you," Alma said.

Sun baked the black-topped parking lot. The truck before the sign had a California license plate. "California, the place you ought to be," Eddie hummed. ("So they loaded up the truck and moved to Beverly.")

He sat on the banana-shaped seat of his bicycle (fake leopard-skin cover). Butter pecan ice cream his favorite, he thought; black raspberry another; also, pistachio, vanilla, orange sherbet, lemon sherbet, maple walnut, strawberry swirl, peach, coffee... He peddled past a saucer-shaped merry-go-round painted in bright yellow and red colors, then past the thick steel poles of the playground swing set.

A red wooden picnic table sat beneath the thick arms of a spreading elm tree beside the cinder-block playground shack.

Mole Bungalatti and Stevie Sondrini sat with heads bowed over a checker board. Mole's younger brother Fred sat on the corner of the table, feet on a bench; he ate a string of red licorice, feeding the string into his mouth like spaghetti. "Forget it, Mole," he said, "you are beat."

Mole held his head in his hands. His black hair combed into a wave-shaped pompadour. "Not yet," he said.

"You will be," moon-faced Sondrini said. "King me."

"Where there is a will there is a way, right Eddie?" Mole said, looking up.

"Mole, you suck at checkers," Fred stated. "I can beat you."

"I can beat YOU," Mole said, holding up a fist. "With this!"

"I will tell Dad," Fred said.

"So what," Mole said, "I am not afraid of him."

"Oh sure!" Fred exclaimed. "I am going to tell him you said that."

"King me!" Sondrini said.

"I was only joking," Mole said. He slammed a checker down on the board.

"Did the Red Sox win last night, Eddie?" Fred asked.

"Got beat. Four to three. Kaline hit a home run. Off of Wyatt."

"The Red Flops will blow it, they always do," Mole said.

"Shut-up, Mole; you will jinx them," Fred said. "They are doing better than anyone thought they would."

Mole lurched upward; Fred scrambled off the table. Fred ran across the playground, Mole in pursuit.

"He will never catch him," Sondrini said.

Eddie smiled; he steered his bike around the table, peddled past the cinder block hut to a cinder track that skirted a deep football field-sized depression in the earth. Eddie wiped his hand on his shirt-front. Cinder crunched beneath the bicycle tires. Shards of golden light speckled the shadowed black pathway, leafy trees like a canopy overhead. Ferns, vines, scrub grass, nettle and picker-bushes lined the pathway. Eddie inhaled the peculiar and unpleasant musky vegetable smell of the swampland.

A fat frog on the cinder path leaped into the brush, flipper-feet attached to little gymnast legs.

Thicker foliage darkened the pathway. Eddie fell a chill in the air. He heard something splash into pooled water in the brush; something big, by the sound of the splash.

The path ended; Eddie peddled onto the cement surface of Old Columbia Street, commonly known as the "back road." He felt glad to leave the swamp behind. He braked and stood in the bright sunshine, straddling the cross bar of the bike. The sun warmed his flesh. He looked across the road to a house that sat high on a knoll. He wondered who lived in the house, now. It was old and falling down; a place new people moved into regularly. The siding of the house warped like wet cardboard. A window in the peak of the roof, boarded with ply-wood.

With a start, he realized he was being watched: a pair of unfriendly eyes in a hostile-looking blunt featured face. The face of an older boy; his head set on the lip of the knoll like a rock. Eddie reached for a pedal with his foot. A strong-looking neck and wide shoulders rose above the lip, the kid's muscular legs and arms churning as he ran down the hill toward the road.

Eddie peeled out, back tire of the bike slipping on the slick road surface.

The guy leaped from the hillside to the street.

Eddie peddled furiously, half-standing, thighs of his legs tightening. He heard the slap-slap-slap of the guy's sneaker-ed feet.

Eddie raced through shadows on the road, past an underground spring that pooled on one side of the street, opposite a drainage ditch full of brackish water. He glanced back.

The guy close behind, his hand reaching for the fender, black eyes like cinders pressed into a dark olive complected face.

Eddie felt his legs burning, sweat rolling from beneath his baseball cap and down his face. He felt the tug of the guy's hand on the seat; he glanced back: the guy stumbled, hand reaching, and gave up, feet slapping to a halt.

Eddie coasted through the sunshine that bathed the road. The guy grew smaller and smaller.

House Call

As the old woman reached for the bottle, she told herself that she had every right in the world to drink.

Every right in the world.

And if she got drunk? SO WHAT! A mother observing the anniversary of a daughter's death had every right in the world to get drunk.

Every right in the world!

She took a healthy slug from the bottle.

If other mothers had her problems, they would drink too, she told herself.

They would drink more than she!

Much more!

Darn tootin' they would!

She looked at the half-full bottle. She had shown self-control by not drinking more than half the bottle. By taking her time. By not guzzling the stuff like some...drunk.

She rewarded her restraint with a stiff drink.

"Poor Rose," she mumbled.

"YES," Frank had said. "ALRIGHT. YES. THANKS FOR CALLING."

The old woman could still hear the click of the telephone as Frank hung up.

"SHE DIED AT FIVE O'CLOCK THIS MORNING."

That was the end of it. She, the old woman, would have visited, she told herself—God knows she would have! But she had had Frank to take care of and the apartment to watch over and other things had come up...So many things...She looked out at the sky hanging like a dirty dish rag over the green landscape of trees and hills.

She took a drink.

Rose was too good anyway, she told herself, for such a stinkin' lousy world. She raised the bottle in memory of Rose—

—the chair tried to contain her, but she broke its grasp and stood, holding her ground, like a sailor on the deck of a ship in a storm. The deck tilted one way then the other. Oopsie! She did a little two-step before bracing herself. She began moving toward a tattered brown couch, taking baby-sized steps. The floor went up and down and she lost her balance and ran head-first into the plaster wall. Her glasses slipped down her nose. She turned, stumbled forward, and belly-flopped onto the couch.

Daylight like a slap of a wet towel hit the old woman. She sat up, blinking. Her head felt as if held in a steel vice-grip. She stared, bleary-eyed, at a figure before her. Could it be, she asked herself. Was it possible? A miracle! Little Rose! Sent by God! Stood on the threadbare carpet wearing a Brownie's uniform of skirt, jersey, and beanie cap. The old woman dropped off the couch onto her knees. She embraced the girl. "Rose!" she bawled, "my baby! My baby girl!"

The Brownie stood like a statue. She looked at the pink-skinned dome of the old woman's skull. The girl's pug nose lifted as she smelled a funny smell—like medicine. The girl tried to back out of the embrace, but the old woman held tight.

"I am not Rose, Grandma," the girl said, "I am Anne."

Fat tears rolled down the grandmother's red-veined purple-splotched cheeks. "My daughter," she bawled into the folds of the skirt. "My BABY!"

The granddaughter looked over her shoulder at another Brownie—smaller, frailer-looking than the granddaughter— standing in the doorway of the living room. The girl's eyes were opened wide, staring.

The grandmother's rheumy eyes, magnified to the size of quarters beneath coke bottle-thick glasses, stared up at the granddaughter. Thin strands of her mop-head of uncombed unwashed hair fell in rivulets down her face. Her jowly flesh sank with disappointment. She moaned and fell face-down to the floor, squealing as she beat the carpet: "Rose! ROSE! R O S E!"

The granddaughter ran to her friend's side. The girls clasped hands and backed into the kitchen of the small apartment, their black & white saddle shoes scraping the linoleum floor.

"What is wrong with her?" the friend asked.

"I don't know. She must be sick."

"Let's go!"

The granddaughter dabbed at an eye with a sleeve. "I think I should call the doctor?"

The girls sat on concrete steps in front of the small two-story wooden house. A paper mill, across the street, blasted a fog-horn blast. Two chipmunks darted from beneath the row of scraggy hedges out front of the yard, their paint brush-like hook-shaped tails upright.

"Is your Grandma going to the hospital?" the friend asked.

"I don't know."

The girls watched as a Cadillac slowed before the house and turned into the narrow driveway.

A middle-aged man with saturnine face topped by wavy brilliantine salt & pepper hair stepped from the car. He wore a white shirt beneath a gray tweed overcoat. Under his arm he carried a football-sized satchel. Walking hunched, as if weighed down by his head, he approached the steps.

"Hello Doctor Baker," the granddaughter said.

"Where is she?" the doctor gruffly demanded. "Upstairs?" He stepped between the girls and pushed open the front door. His shiny black oxfords punched the rungs of the wooden staircase.

He strode into the apartment.

The old woman lay on the floor like a beached seal.

"Get up off the floor," the doctor shouted. "What are you doing on the floor? Do you sleep on the floor now?"

The old woman rose to her feet and stumbled onto the couch, a crescent of white slip hanging below her wrinkled gray dress.

"Look at yourself! Just LOOK at yourself! Noon-time, and in this condition!" A scowl darkened the doctor's olive-face. He dropped his satchel onto an end table. "It is disgraceful!"

The doctor flung an arm out toward the girls, standing in the doorway. "Look what you are doing to your little grand-daughter and her friend! You are no good," he shouted. "No good to your family—no damn good to anyone!" He dug into the satchel. "You ought to be ashamed!"

"I am; I am, doctor; but I miss my Rose—my girl!"

"Rose is dead," the doctor stated, "and she is going to stay dead. And that is no excuse for you to put your husband, and your granddaughter, through this sort of treatment!"

The doctor's shoes slid along the carpet as he gesticu-lated. "Why don't you think of someone else beside yourself? Think about what you are doing to your family—to the people around you. For once! For once in your life, try that!"

The doctor rattled two pills in his hand. "Get me a glass of water," he ordered the granddaughter, who jumped to obey.

"I will, doctor," the old woman whined. "Believe me, I will!" She plucked the pills from the doctor's hand. "Thank you, doctor."

The doctor snatched the glass of water from the granddaughter. "Never mind 'thank you.' If you do not want to go back to the hospital you had better straighten out!" He slapped the satchel shut with a two-handed clout.

"You people disgust me," he said. "I am sick of dealing with you; sick of watching you ruin your lives and the lives of those around you." He threw his arm out toward the girls. "Just look! Look what you are—"

The arm stopped mid-swing, finger pointing to the empty doorway.

Turmoil

HAWK-NOSED Leno Decensi gnawed a chunk off the butt end of a foot-long stick of pepperoni then threw the stick back into the refrigerator and swung the door shut. He chewed with eyes at half-mast, a channel of pain through his head, temple to temple, like someone had driven a railroad spike through. A patter of small feet pounded the kitchen floor like a drum solo playing inside Leno's head. His twin brothers, Peter and Pauly, ran past him into the living room and crashed to the floor in a heap. "Knock it off!" Leno commanded. The twins looked up, white faces flushed. Leno groaned, walked across the kitchen linoleum to the table in a corner. A copy of the NY DAILY NEWS next to an ashtray full of stamped-out cigarette butts. H R HALDEMAN ON HOT SEAT, Leno read. DID PREZ KNOW OF COVERUP? Leno pushed the paper aside. A copy of TRUE DETECTIVE magazine lay underneath. The hot tangy sting of pepperoni burnt at the base of Leno's throat; he picked up the magazine, brought the cover to within an inch of his thick glasses. Scanned the cover with quick side-to-side head movements. A buxom blonde being raped by a muscular knife-wielding maniac. The blonde's blouse half torn off. Leno wished the artist had shown the blouse completely off. A knock at the front door sounded like a punch. Leno dropped the magazine, walked to the window, pushed the drawn curtain aside. Blinked and stared. The lump of pepperoni slid down his throat like a rock.

"Be right there! Keep your pants on!" Leno took deep breaths. Stepped and opened the door. A cop, seven feet tall, in a black uniform. Two moles on the cop's hairless face. A nose like a baked potato.

"Is your name Decensi? Leno Decensi? Leno B. Decensi?"

The cop had a turtle shell-shaped pot belly. His thumbs hooked into his service belt.

"Yea, that's right. Don't wear it out."

The cop stared. "Mind if I ask you a few questions?" The cop rested a palm on top of his holstered revolver.

Leno gazed from the gun to the cop's head. His black cap had a silver star above the visor. The cap rested on the back of a pin-shaped skull. "Alright," Leno agreed, "but make it snappy. I left the bathtub running." He hooked a thumb over his shoulder. "I mean, I mean I left the water running." He felt a smile creeping over his face.

"This ain't no joke, Decensi."

"I know it's not." A laugh burst from Leno like a hiccup.

The cop stared with eyes like painted hard-boiled eggs. Leno's teeth, sticking out of his gums at odd angles, looked like the teeth of a baby shark, the cop reflected. A wad of white adhesive tape, on the bridge of the kid's nose, held his black-rimmed glasses together. "Where was you last night?"

Leno stared at the cop's black Buster Brown shoes. "I don't remember."

"Well, start remembering!"

"The Oasis Lounge," Leno stated.

The cop pulled a stubby pencil from behind his ear and wrote in a notebook. "Was you there all night?"

"Yeah, all night—then I come straight home."

The cop's eyebrows arched. "I didn't ask if you come straight home."

"Well, I'm telling you. I'm being cooperative." Leno shrugged. "I'm a cooperative kind of guy; that's the way I am. Besides, I got nothin' to hide because I didn't do nothin'!"

The kid was odd, the cop thought; maybe even a little touched in the head. No respect for authority at all. The kind of bird who WOULD drive an automobile over a golfing green. "Well, if you got nothin' to hide, then you don't mind me takin' a picture or two, do you?"

Leno blinked. "Picture? What is this," he smirked, brow furrowed above the tape, "DRAGNET?"

"Just a look around. After all, a guy like you, wid' nothin' to hide...that's the troot, right?"

"Go ahead," Leno insisted, waving an arm. "Look around! It's a free country! But you won't find nothin'—that I guar-RAUN-tee," he drawled.

"Where is your car, Decensi?"

"Huh? I ain't got one."

"How about your mother and father—where's their car?"

"They ain't got one either. We're too poor. We're hoping President Nixon repeals the child labor laws so my younger brothers can go to work."

The cop clenched his fist. Bugged by the talk of the smart-mouthed wise-ass. A good smack in the puss might do the kid some good, he thought. Change the kid's attitude...The cop felt his heart pounding. He gritted his teeth. Felt sweat gather on his scalp. His blood pressure, he knew, must be sky high. He slid his hand down into his front pocket, felt for his nitro pills. A sweat crept over his forehead. He must have left the pills on his kitchen counter...(Hell with the wise-ass, and the golfing green—crisscrossed with tire-sized divots). "Well," he said, "I'll be talking to you, Decensi."

"Oh yea? Sure!" Leno eagerly agreed. "Why not? Alright, see you later, Bugsy!" Leno swung the door shut.

"Ha-Ha!" Pauly Decensi, squatting beneath the kitchen table, mimicked a laugh. "Leno's going to jail-ail," he sing-song-ed.

"Shut-up! I am not!" Leno ran up the staircase, feet pounding the rungs. Moved down a carpeted hallway to the front bedroom. Looked out at the cop, pointing a camera at tire tracks in the driveway

shitShitSHIT

why did he not make the cop get a search warrant?

The cop got into an unmarked black car. The car reminded Leno of a hearse.

Dotti Decensi stabbed her Virginia Slims Extra Long Menthol cigarette into the glass ashtray on the kitchen table. "PETER!" she screeched. "PAULY! YOUSE BASTARDS KNOCK IT OFF, YOUSE HEAR ME? I SAID KNOCK IT OFF FOR CRISE SAKE YOU'RE DRIVIN' ME FRICKIN' BATTY!"

She twirled a strand of hair around her finger. Studied the magazine spread on the table.

WILLIE MAYS IS WHITE, she read.

A crash on the other side of the staircase brought Dottie's head snapping up. "KNOCK IT OFF I SAID!! YOUSE WANT ME COME IN THERE AND RIP YOUR GOD-DAMN HEADS OFF?" Dotti launched herself, bounding around the staircase that separated kitchen and living room. "WHAT THE CRISE DID I TELL YOUSE? KNOCK THIS SHIT OFF, YOUSE HEAR ME? WHAT I GOTTA DO, WRITE YOUSE A GODDAMN LETTER?"

The twins peeked at Dottie from behind an over-stuffed easy chair. Twelve-year old Louie, lying on the couch, caught the rubber ball—the ball he had been throwing against a wall behind the TV set—in the palm of his hand. Dottie glared, oval lenses of her glasses perched on her hawk-like nose. Nosecones of her breasts thrust like bullets beneath a sleeveless brown polyester jersey. "YOU GODDAMN KIDS ARE DRIVIN' ME TO THE BUGHOUSE! KNOCK THIS SHIT OFF, NOW!"

Louie rolled onto his side, reached to the black short-haired barrel-chested dog beside the couch. Gilligan, of GILLIGAN'S ISLAND, argued with the Skipper. The Skipper tore his hat off, threw the cap to the ground. Louie leaned down, wrapped the dog's head in his arms, and kissed the beast on its thin purple lips.

Disgust darkened Dottie's smooth-skinned harried-looking face. She stalked around the staircase, pointing a finger back toward the living room: "TOMORROW I'M PUTTING ALL OF YOUSE UP FOR ADOPTION! I'M NOT SHITTIN' YOUSE EITHER!" She marched to the table, her white deck sneakers scraping the linoleum floor, fabric of her clinging brown polyester stretch pants rasping across the inside of her thighs. She tore open a new pack of cigarettes and lit up. Louie bounced the ball off the wall; the twins fell to the floor in a clinch; the Skipper bellowed, "GILLIGAN!" Dotti sent a stream of white smoke out over the table; the smoke floated into the shape of a distant mountain range. She flipped the page of her magazine.

LIBERACE NOT GAY

Beneath the headline a photo of Liberace in a jewel-studded suit, cape flung about his shoulders, white incisors displayed in a rapacious-looking smile. Dotti looked approvingly at the outfit. Wondered what it cost. Probably more than her goddamn house. She did not care if he was gay or sad or whatever...She wished she had some of his money, though. If she did have some, she'd get on an airplane, she told herself, and head to Hawaii. Sit on the beach and drink My-Ties. Look at surfer-boys. Quit her stinkin' job too—after telling her boss to kiss her ass—then maybe have somebody put some sheet-rock up over the exposed wiring and bare walls of the house...

Soles of Leno's high-cut brown hush puppy shoes slapped the wooden rungs of the staircase. "What's all the noise? You woke me up." He cupped a hand over a yawn.

"Leno! My baby!" Dottie stretched her arms out. "Come give your mother a big hug!"

"Go'wan," Leno muttered, blushing. "What's for din-din?" He strode across the kitchen, scratching beneath his tight white t-shirt.

"Meatloaf," Dottie said. "LOUIE! GODDAMN YOU! TURN THAT TV DOWN BEFORE I SMASH IT!"

"Meatloaf again?"

"Yea, it is all I can afford on the money your asshole father gives me."

Leno let the stove door slam shut. He walked to the refrigerator, opened the door, picked up a can of Viennese pickled sausage. "Why don't you take him back to court?" He pinched a sausage from the can.

"I oughta! No good bastard gives all his money to that whore he lives with—doesn't even care if his own goddamn children starve or not."

Leno read the label of the sausage can, holding the can up to his glasses.

"He is not getting his F-en book back either," Dottie said.

"What book?"

"The black notebook he left in the closet—with all his tax records in it. He thinks he's coming over here and taking it, but he's not.

"I don't care if the I.R.S. is on his ass—that is his problem, not mine. He should have paid his taxes, like everyone else. Let him go to jail, what do I give a shit? It's where he belongs!"

Leno wondered if the old man would ask him to retrieve the book. Wondered how much money the book might be worth.

"And don't go giving it to him!"

"HON-ie! You know I wouldn't!" Leno walked to the table.

"Yea, well...don't."

Leno massaged Dotti's shoulders.

Dottie lowered her head. "Oh, that's good, yea! Right there!"

Leno kneaded the flesh: flesh of his flesh.

Dottie swiveled her head. "What did you do to my car, anyway? It's filthy!"

"Don't worry," Leno cooed. "I'm going to take the car and wash it. Do the inside too."

Dottie's head sunk. "Do the neck too, will you?"

Leno pressed down on the accelerator and the big V-8 engine purred like a big cat. The Chevy roared down Howling Avenue, past small wooden houses and rickety-looking tenement blocks dotting the roadside. Brown billy-club shaped cattails in the scummy water of a swampy field to Leno's left, at the base of the gently rolling mountainside. Leno watched the speedometer move to within 5 miles an hour of his Howling Avenue straightaway speed record. A car pulled out of Gray Street, fifty yards ahead of Leno. He jammed the brake and glided to within a yard of the Gray Street nitwit. A trailer truck in the opposite lane rumbled past trailing a cloud of dust. Leno punched the steering wheel with the heel of his palm. An orange highway department dump truck rattled past in the wake of the trailer truck. The silver-haired woman in the car ahead of Leno glanced up: her mouth dropped open, eyes wide in the rear-view mirror. Leno grinned, inched the Chevy further to his left and stomped on the accelerator. "Park it, you old biddy!" he screamed, as he sped past.

White dust covered the highway like a sheet across the road. Lime kiln buildings thickly coated with the white paste of ossified lime waste looked like vanilla double and triple tiered cakes. Churning masses of smoke rose roiling into the blue sky, above the cakes.

The car slid on the iron railroad tracks cutting diagonally across the pavement. Leno turned the car with the slide and the Chevy came out of it's fishtail. Leno glanced in the mirror at a white dust cloud he left behind. He felt proud. After glimpsing disaster, he had unflappably fought his way out like a champion. Like Mario Andretti, or Strling Moss, he told himself. A hump in the road jolted him upright. "Yee-hah!" he shouted.

The Chevy dropped down an incline and onto another straightaway. Straddling the double yellow lines in the road, Leno debated whether to try and pass half a dozen cars ahead. He forced a small compact car in the opposite lane into the thin breakdown lane. Leno smirked at the gutless ninny behind the wheel. Behind the compact, a cement mixer, the driver sitting in the cab as if on a throne. Leno turned the wheel of the Chevy to avoid being pinioned on the mixer's front end. He glanced at the truck in the rear-view mirror. Felt admiration for the driver. He flicked the radio on, whistled off-key to the fluted notes of "To the Hustle." Sniffed the stench of gas and oil from the service station to his left. Up Your Ass With Mobil Gas! He braked, turned, and brought the car to a screeching halt at curbside. "Hey! Murf!" he shouted. "What's cookin'?"

Short, compact, and broad-shouldered Murf, standing beneath the awning of ANGIE'S SUB SHOP, smiled. He walked to the car. A jumbo-sized pickle, wrapped in white butcher's paper, clutched in his hand.

"Hop in," Leno said.

Murf sat.

"What's shakin', Murf?"

Murf bit into the pickle, spraying pickle juice over the dashboard. "Bunch of bullshit." He chewed, pale blue eyes in a pimpled face surveying the road.

"Oh yea?" Leno steered one-handed, left arm out the window and lying against the door. "So gimme the skinny. What's the turmoil?"

"My brother. I come home last night, and you know what he done?"

"What?"

Murf rested a muscular bicep on the door frame. "He smashed all my albums and piled them on the floor."

"No!" Leno smiled, side-glanced Murf to see if Murf caught the smile. "What's his malfunction?"

"Because I did not get the car back in time for him to take it to work. He had to ride with one of his asshole friends."

Leno stared at a woman pushing a baby carriage in front of the A & P Market. "So, what did you do about the albums?"

"I tore all his books in half."

Leno laughed. Teeth sticking out like pegs hammered in by a rough-carpenter.

Murf wadded the butcher's paper. "Where to?"

"The car wash. You see all the crap on the car? Got to get it off before the cops see it. Suckerface Jonesy, the Detective, was at my house this morning."

"No shit? For what?"

"Wait 'til I tell you," Leno grinned.

Leno pulled the Chevy out of the car-wash yard, spinning tires kicking up a storm cloud of dust and rocks. Dust motes of the cloud sparkled in the sunlight. Tires squealed onto asphalt.

"Flatfoots can't pin anything on me now!" Leno said.

"Where to?" Murf asked.

"Why don't you come back to the ranch? Dorothea has a meatloaf cooking—plus I'll cook up a mess of scrambled eggs and un-yoans...Later we can go out for a few teas."

"OK," Murf said, with heightened interest. He looked out the window at PLUNKETT Junior High School, brown-bricked, multi-windowed, three stories with slate roof capped with gables, turrets; he thought of long dark corridors in sepia tones; footsteps and shadows in the corridors...

The Chevy roared through the blinking red light of North Main Street, tires squealing on the turn. On the corner, an old man flinched, looking quickly to the road. Leno grinned, shifted the car into neutral and revved the engine. Coasted behind a line of traffic. A cop standing with arms crossed, beside the black lollipop-shaped BRIGHTON SAVINGS BANK clock, sullenly stared.

"Big man," Murf said, staring at the short square-shouldered cop.

"Boxing champion," Leno said. "I'd like to know who he fought. Probably some guy with multiple sclerosis." Leno shifted: car tires barked. He laughed. "You see his face?"

"Yea!" Murf studied the contour of his arm in the side mirror. "Wonder how tough he is without the gun?"

"You could beat the shit out of him. Half the guys he fought were probably from the Oasis Lounge—stiffer than old shoes."

Murf looked up at the shiny black stone face of William McKinley, Friend of Brighton, standing twenty feet high on a platform of pink Italian marble, the President's right arm extended in a stiff-arming gesture. "Yea, guys with half-a-bag on," Murf said. "Hey, look. There is Big Lean."

Thin lanky Big Lean stood beside a white van parked on the street in front of Val's Variety store. Black letters on the side of the van read DECENSI ELECTRIC. Big Lean waved.

"What's new, boy?" Big Lean shouted, striding to the driver's side window of the Chevy.

Big Lean hung his arms on the roof. He wore a white t-shirt, blue jeans, and unlaced work boots. His swarthy complexion coupled with a pencil-line thin black mustache gave him the look of a Mexican bandito. His bald head was covered by a film of hair combed over the dome of his skull. "Murphy!" he called, craggy face drifting inside the car, "how you doin', Murphy?"

Murf nodded, grinned.

"Look what your Democrats are doin' to President Nixon, Murphy! The best President this country ever had, and they want to kick him out! Can you beat it? It ain't right, I tell you, and it's all the Democrats doin'! Those Democrats are no good, Murphy! Them bastards are no good I tell you! None of 'em!" Big Lean's face darkened. "Including the one we got—that Kennedy! Yah, Kennedy! He killed that girl there, and what happened to him? Nothin'! Not a goddamn thing!"

"Tricky Dicky," Murf said, "his goose is cooked!"

"Tax and spend!" Big Lean shouted. "That's all your Democrats do, them bastards!" He glanced suspiciously to his right, at a passing car. "Leno, listen to me, Leno; I need you do me a favor—it's important. Are you listening?"

"I'm all ears," Leno said, smirking.

"I need you to get a book for me—a black notebook in the downstairs closet. On the top shelf. You get it for me, you hear? You hear me, boy?"

"Sure. Twenty bucks."

"Twenty! Like hell!" Big Lean glared. "After all I done for you?" he whined. "All I give you? Took you skiing up to Jiminy Peak, bought you a Boston Patriots jacket...Five dollars!"

"Twenty."

"No! Not twenty! Ten!"

"Fifteen. Final offer."

"Why you goddamn shyster, you're worse than a goddamn Jew! Where did you learn to act like this? Not from me you didn't! Must have been from Dottie! Dottie taught you to act like this, didn't she?"

Leno put the car into gear, started forward. "Take it or leave it!"

Big Lean walked alongside the car. "You rotten bastard," he shouted as Leno pulled away from the curb.

"Jeremiah was a bullfrog," the jukebox bawled. "He was a good friend of mine!"

Murf stared at an empty shot glass before him on the table. "Another one?" he said.

"Sure," Leno agreed, "you got the coin?"

Murf wedged a thick hand into a front pocket of his dungaree shorts.

Smoke floated over the half dozen men sitting at the bar. The bartender sat behind the bar on a stool and read the BRIGHTON TRANSCRIPT.

WATERGATE INVESTIGATION CONTINUES

Above the bartender, on the screen of the TV in the corner, crew-cut, hard-eyed, White House Chief of Staff H. R. Haldeman's lips moved forming silent words.

"Nothin'," Murf said glumly. He wedged the shot glass into his eye like a monocle.

"Deke," Leno pleaded, "buy a round."

Deke stared, glassy-eyed. A green cotton Army fatigue cap sat atop his huge cinder-block-shaped head. "I bought five rounds," he complained in his high-pitched voice. "I ain' got enough left for a free lunch."

"Sprechenen-zee-Deutsch?" Murf asked.

Deke giggled and a line of drool ran down the prognathous jaw of his broad face.

Leno began swinging his shoulders side-to-side, head bent. He punched himself in the chest. "Heartburn," he croaked.

"Nothin' but a bunch of crooks!" a red-faced old man yelled up at the TV. "And Nixon is the biggest of the bunch!"

"Relax," the young bartender said.

"I'll relax you, you punk," the old man said.

"Let's go the Oasis!" Murf said. He lurched from his chair. "The Oasis!" he shouted. He goose-stepped across the butt-strewn floor and kicked the front door open.

The night was warm, air soft like velvet on Murf's skin. He walked into a parking meter.

Deke ducked his head, stepping from the bar.

A full moon shone bright as a light bulb.

Murf howled.

Leno pissed a golden stream that splattered the sidewalk.

Deke laughed walking up the sidewalk, a flat-footed trudge, soles of his unlaced work boots scraping cement.

A cop car pulled out of the dark of a parking lot across the street. The bubble light of the cruiser splashed fluorescent blue light over trees, cars, buildings...A cop jumped from the cruiser. "Hold it right there!"

Deke teetered like a tree in a wind storm. "Hello, Ossifer!"

A flashlight painted Deke's face yellow. His eyes looked like two puddles.

"Where to, Bub?" The short square-shouldered cop looked up at Deke.

Deke giggled.

"What are you a fuckin' comedian?"

Deke's teeth gleamed between blubbery lips.

"What you got in your pocket?"

Deke dipped fingers into his t-shirt pocket. Displayed an empty shot glass.

"Stole it, huh? Stole it from that bar."

Leno stepped up to the cop. "He found it. On the railroad tracks."

Another cop, taller, less compact than his partner, played his flashlight over Leno.

"What's up, Bugsy?"

"So, you found it, is 'dat the story? 'Dat right?"

"I don't know," Deke squeaked. Drool ran down his chin.

"What is your name?"

"Ralph," Deke said.

"Ralph who?"

"Ralph Kramden."

"Alright—you're coming with us! Get in the car!"

"WHAT? He didn't do nothin'!" Leno barked. "You can't arrest him!"

"Oh no?"

"NO! He didn't do nothin' wrong!"

The taller cop grasped Deke's arm. Deke lumbered to the cruiser.

"You want to come wid' us?" the short cop said.

Leno stared.

"Big man," Murf said as the cop moved to the car.

"Yea, real big. Who'd he fight, a double amputee?" Leno ran to the side of the cruiser. Deke looked out the back window. "We'll get you out! Don't sweat it! They can't do anything to you!"

The cruiser drove off, leaving behind a stench of exhaust fumes.

Dottie Decensi, beached on the living room couch like a seal, snored with mouth opened. A short thick arm protruded like a ship's rudder from the couch. Under the arm a pile of magazines, cut and torn, pages scattered in shreds across the floor. Beside the magazines, a pair of long-sheared scissors. Beside the scissors an empty can of Chocolate Fudge Low-Cal Diet soda. The television cast a lurid glow in the dark room, black and white ants scrambling across the screen, fighting their night-long war.

Dottie's hand flailed the air, pulling back on the oar of the boat, the rowing a real chore for her as the handles of the oars were too thick for her to securely grasp. How the boat continued to glide so smoothly across the blue sea was a mystery to her.

A yacht three stories high passed, moving in the opposite direction. People on the yacht's deck bent over the railing, staring down at her. Laughing at her. Her asshole boss from the factory; ex-husband Big Lean (with his girlfriend the hair-dressing whore); and Liberace. "Look at that dumb bastard,"

Big Lean said, nudging Liberace. The hairdressing whore laughed gaily. "You'd think she would have some sheet-rock up, in this day and age," Liberace said.

HAWAII printed in black letters on the yacht's side.

Leno, Louie, Peter, and Pauly jumped from the yacht and each hit the water like a cannonball and sunk. Dottie jumped overboard to save them and

was in a dark room, sitting on a bed. The bed creaked when she moved. The door of the room slowly swung open. It was her parent's bed, she realized with a start. She was in the old house where she had grown up. A noise on the staircase outside the room disturbed her. Some one or thing coming up the stairs, step by step, rung by rung. Ever closer. Closer...A big black shadow appeared in the doorway and

Dottie woke, staring up at the ceiling. Her heart thumped thump thump—what a freakin' dream! She listened to the static of the TV. Felt comforted by the sound. Kicked her blanket off and sat up, bare feet barely touching the floor. Tugged her nightgown over plump thighs. A quizzical expression on her face. Backyard crickets began to squawk like spectators at a football game. How many crickets did it take, she wondered, to make such an ungodly racket? "Goddamnit," she said, suddenly sitting upright. An odd sound—a soft "schusssch" from beyond the couch end...Outside? A dog or squirrel sniffing around? She caught her breath up. DAMNIT! Someone opening the pantry window! Jimmying the thing up by degrees. Who in hell...

SON OF A BITCH. BASTARD. Had to be him! Going to get his book. Waltz right in and take it!

She clenched her hands; lips shut like a steel trap.

The living room began to pulse in time with the thumping of her heart. Blood rushed like flood waters to her head. A red-tinted haze turned the room into a cloudy inferno. Dots on the TV screen began to arrange themselves into symbols, signs, announcing a message, a message she could not ignore. Snatching up the scissors, she stepped down the couch to the edge of the pantry. The bastard had the window halfway up, the silhouette of his features clear against the moon-bright sky. A long jean-covered leg slithered through the window opening, the boot on the foot probing for the floor. Dottie raised the scissors above her head. Big Leans' thigh lay like a loaf of bread on the window sill. Dottie stepped forward and stabbed.

The bald middle-aged police sergeant held his hands palms upward in a helpless gesture. "Like I said, 'dat's the law, boys!" Fluorescent overhead lights cast ping-pong ball-sized shadows beneath the sergeant's eyes, nose and mouth. A short wave radio behind the station desk crackled with static, voices coming in and fading out. "He's here for 'da night. He'll be free to go in 'da morning. In 'da morn-ning," he sing-songed.

"How about personal recognizance?" Murf asked, face red and sweat-slicked, arms folded on the countertop.

"Yea, how about it?" Leno said, nodding to Murf. "About what he said."

"Never heard of it," the sergeant said. "Ain't no such animal."

"Like hell there ain't! Listen, Bugsy–" Leno pointed a finger at the cop's face. "You got no right to keep him here—none! He didn't do nothin' wrong!"

"We got the right to keep anyone we want. Doin' wrong got nothin' to do wid' it."

"WHAT? What are you saying?" Leno demanded.

"We do what we want," the sergeant stated, "and we want him in here, and you, and YOU, out there! Now get out! The both of youse!"

"What about habeas corpus?" Murf said. "What about the Constitution? The Declaration of Independence!"

Leno pounded his fist on the desk top. "JUSTICE!" he screamed. "We want justice! We want him out, now! NOW! You hear me? NOW!"

The sergeant's cheek twitched.

"THE CHARGE?" Leno hollered. "WHAT IS THE CHARGE? WHAT DID HE DO? TELL ME! ON WHAT CHARGE? TELL ME!..."

The front door of the station opened: the short cop and his partner walked in.

"...SHOW ME! Show me the law that says what you say! I want to see it!" Leno hammered the desk top. "Now! NOW!"

A stout dog-faced cop and a tall cop with an altar-boy's face entered the room from an alcove right of the desk. The dog-faced cop grabbed Murf's wrist and twisted Murf's arm back. Murf walked ahead of the cop to the alcove doorway and into the cell area.

"Come on!" Leno urged the desk sergeant. "Show me the law where it says..." Leno glanced back then turned, staring in surprise at the cops around him. He yanked his arm free of the grasp of the altar-boy-faced cop. "Keep your fucking hands off me." The short square-shouldered cop rushed Leno. Leno kicked the cop between the legs. The cop collapsed in a heap on the floor. The sergeant lunged over the counter and wrapped an arm around Leno's neck. The altar-boy-faced cop and the short square-shouldered cop's partner plowed into Leno, knocking him back against the desk. Reaching up, Leno raked the sergeant's face, opening a gash on the cop's cheek. The short square-shouldered cop's partner cracked his billy-club off Leno's head. The radio screeched. Blood ran down the sergeant's face and onto Leno's scalp. Leno slid down the face of the desk, kicking his feet out as if riding a bicycle. "Son's a bitches!" he screamed. The stout dog-faced cop pointed a can of mace at Leno's face and sprayed. Leno screamed, jerking convulsively, like a puppet pulled by strings. The dog-faced cop lay across Leno's legs as the short square-shouldered cop laboriously crawled up onto Leno and straddled his chest. The cop began punching. The punches splat splat splat on Leno's face; he threw his head side-to-side, tasting blood pooling in his mouth. He soon stopped feeling the punches, his face numb, frozen. He spit a mouthful of blood and teeth...

The overhead lights of the station began to dim.

Pistol

He woke fully dressed, lying in his bed, arms outstretched like a man crucified. A window shade beside the bed rose on a breeze, crinkled and flapped like a big tongue tasting the air. He winced at the sound. The daylight hurt his eyes; he swung his thin legs off the bed and sat up. Whoa! The room turned: a clockwise motion then back again, as if adjusting itself. He shut his eyes, bracing himself with hands on the mattress.

The door of the room flew open.

"Louis!"

His mother, wearing a terrycloth bathrobe, red, like a campfire. "WHERE IS THE CAR?" she shouted.

"Jesus Christ," Louie said, rubbing his forehead. "In the drive."

"It is NOT in the drive!"

He listened to his mother's feet beat across the floor like drums.

Louie stared at a crack in the linoleum. The car? He heard footsteps approaching like an army on the march.

Louie teetered to his feet. His father and mother stood in the doorway. His father wore a white t-shirt; his face blue with stubble, nose red, and a vein in the middle of his forehead swollen like a night-crawler..."What did do with the car?" he screamed. "YOU CRACK IT UP? ANSWER ME!"

Louie blinked; shrugged his shoulders.

The fucking car.

Louie's father stepped across the room and threw a Rocky Marciano right-hook.

Louie ducked the punch and the room ducked with him up and down. He ran to the door and out, past his mother, who rabbit-punched him in the ear as he ran past.

"GODDAMN DRUNK!" his father screamed.

The cool morning air burnt Louie's throat. He sucked air for breath. "Oh my christ," he said…He walked along the sidewalk and over a truck-long bridge, spanning a river in the trough of cement retaining walls. The river giggled. It thought him funny, Louie told himself.

The smell of grease and fried chicken assailed his big nose. Three cars in the lot of KENTUCKY FRIED CHICKEN across the street. A seagull flew over the roof of the joint; a french fry like fangs in the bird's mouth…In the park beside the river trees stood, bare, branches raised like arms in some kind of beseeching action. When did the trees lose their leaves, Louie wondered. He gazed at cars in Goldman's Super-Duper Market parking lot. Traffic noise revved like an engine inside his head. FIND THE CAR, he told himself. The goddamn car. A cat-sized crow stood in the sidewalk, looking, to Louie, pissed-off, and as if daring him to pass. He kicked at the bird, wondering if the thing would attack him. The crow flew off, croaking, "ut oh! Ut oh!"

Louie's mouth felt dry, like a desert. Should have grabbed a quart of milk from the frig before he booked, he thought. He searched his pockets for his money. SHIT! Where did his money go? He must have been robbed! Or did he lose it? He leaned against a telephone pole and watched cars pass. Too bad he did not have a cigarette, he thought. Or a joint. The pole smelled like tar and resin.

A vague memory, distant, like the First World War, came into his mind. A booth in CHICK'S Lounge and two girls sitting across from him. A blonde and a red-head. The blonde had big knockers. The red-head pretty and with silver nose ring. He recalled the feel of the redhead's lips, the smell of shampoo in her hair...She was married, he remembered her saying. Married! And had kids...Three or four or...The memory faded.

A truck ground a couple pounds worth of gears. The truck driver had a mountain-man beard and a tortured look on his face. Angry eyes in a melon-sized head. The eyes looked down onto Louie, who flinched. The red-head's husband, he told himself. Holy shit! Drops of sweat sprouted on his scalp and rolled down his back like rain. It could not be, he thought. Or, could it?

He walked hurriedly, looking back once before he reached the corner. Run like a bastard, he told himself, if the guy came after him. Could he run like a bastard, he wondered. His feet felt as if someone had pounded nails into his soles.

An old lady driving past in a Cadillac gave him a fishy-eyed look. Louie wondered what her problem was: lose her false teeth?

Behind the Caddy, a pick-up truck: the guy driving pointed his index finger like a gun out the window. Louie cringed. Chooch Rondini—who tended bar at CHICK'S—stuck his peanut-shaped head out the truck window: "PISTOL!" he shouted.

Louie hated the name. John the bartender at the American Legion tagged him with it and it had stuck. He did not want to be "Pistol," but he was...Maybe the car is at the Legion, he thought; he crossed the street as a guy with sun-burnt face and pointy van Dyke beard walked out of AL'S Hardware carrying a pitchfork. Louie moved quickly aside: for some reason, he could not explain, the guy gave him, Louie, the creeps.

Church bells tolled BONG Bong bong bong bong bong
"Jesus!" Louie said, cupping his ears.

Birds like ashes fluttered around the steeple of the church. Sky above smoky gray.

A whale-sized fire truck rolled out of the fire station and wallowed in the street, lights flashing red and yellow, siren wailing like a signal for the end of the world.

"Bastard!" Louie shouted.

The truck took its sweet time going to douse the flames.

Louie read the marquee above the movie theater entrance: LOST IN SPACE, A Romanical Comedy Out of This World, Starring Tipsy Hedron and Nipsy Russell.

He nearly walked into a bow-legged man wearing a homburg and carrying a big fish under his arm. The fishes mouth flapped open and closed, as if it were trying to speak. The distant siren of the fire truck wailed.

The black eyes of a red brick tenement block across the street stared down at Louie who became self-conscious under the scrutiny. He studied the cracks in the cement sidewalk; got a whiff of the odor of burning meat and glanced through the window of MISS BRIGHTON DINER. An old crone gnawed a hunk of bloody meat that looked, to Louie, like a baby's arm. He shivered and looked away; noticed a big basket of bread loaves in the window of SCHWARTZ Sporting Goods Store; wondered since when did Schwartzie start selling bread? A sign on the door of PETE'S Market read BUY FISH...Fuck fish, Louie thought. He wanted something to drink, like a Pepsi, or a can of Budweiser.

He heard the puth puth puth of a car engine and then the squeal of brakes. He glanced at his brother's black Volkswagen

Beetle, nose to the curbside. His brother jumped from the car. He wore a gray sweatshirt and pants. A red bandanna tied around his head. "Where is Dad's car?" he shouted. Louie backed away, trying to escape the aroma of bad breath as his brother's eagle-eyes bore into his. "Hey, why don't you go run some laps, or something?" Louie said. His brother's fist felt like a blunt end of a stick hitting his, Louie's, face. The sidewalk underneath his rear end was cold; he watched his brother walk away.

The car made farting noises as it sped off. Louie touched his lip, swollen like a rubber inner tube. He stood and walked to the curbside. Watched cars pass. Threw a hand up at a Chevy Explorer Wagon in the lane opposite. The driver of the Chevy nodded. Louie stepped into the street, over a dead fish, silver with glossy pink and turquoise sheen, lying in the gutter. A car passed in front of him like a hot breeze. Louie wiped sweat from his face with his shirt sleeve.

The Chevy idled at curbside, the driver's head level with the car's dashboard; silky hair capped the head like an over-turned bowl.

"Mouse!" Louie called, approaching. "What are you doing, Mouse?"

Mouse shrugged. "Nothin'," he said, like a complaint.

Louie dodged a tractor trailer rig loaded with cars.

"What happened to your lip?" Mouse asked, staring.

"My brother punched me."

"Is that right?" Mouse looked amused.

"Can you help me, Mouse?" Louie pleaded.

"With what?"

"Help me look for my father's car. I lost it."

Mouse's big square white teeth gleamed in his kid-sized face. "What do you mean, 'lost it'?"

"What do you mean, what do I mean? I can't find it!"

"No shit," Mouse said.

"No shit."

Mouse glanced at a passing car. "Sixty-seven Mustang," he said.

"Help me look, will you?" Louie begged.

"The silver ElDorado," Mouse said.

"Yeah."

Mouse went into deep thought as he watched cars. Louie waited. The mountainside rose like a vast brown wall behind the church. Something half-way up the church steeple caught Louie's eye: a golden cherubim, swaddled in cloths, and clinging to the spire of the steeple. The cherubim waved a chubby hand in Louie's direction.

"Hop in," Mouse said, decisively.

Louie sat. Mouse fiddled with the radio, tuning-in The Righteous Brothers singing "you lost that loving feeling."

Mouse stared ahead over the dashboard as the car moved down the street. "Whoa oh oh oh," he sang, "whoa oh oh oh."

Louie looked at parked cars. Did he really just see an angel wave to him, he wondered. An angel on the church steeple... Waving??

"Hey!" said Mouse, looking up into the rear view mirror, "I think your father's car just went by!"

Louie swiveled his head to the Chevy's rear window.

"I'm pretty sure," Mouse said. "Some girl driving."

"A red-head?" Louie asked.

Theater

Murphy put on his gray checkered suit, a high school graduation present from his grandmother, over a pink shirt. He left the top two shirt buttons undone. The unbuttoned style of cool guys and snappy dressers, he thought; and he knew that he should be snappily dressed to attend the theater. He had a hard time with that word: "theater." Was it "thee-a-trr," or "thee-ate-er"? He slipped his feet into his platform heeled shoes and his height shot up three inches. In the mirror above the bedroom bureau he looked, he told himself, worldly, even sophisticated-like—like a guy who hung around theaters, maybe—who maybe even wrote a few plays himself.

His heels knocked on the hallway tile floor. The living room, at the end of the hall, was the largest of the clean three room apartment. His brother Al, asleep on the living room couch, snored.

He, Murphy, was in luck, he told himself.

His grandmother sat in a rocking chair before the color television; she turned her head as he approached. "Well!" she exclaimed, "what are you all dolled-up for?" Her ivory dentures showed in a smile. Little squares of light, from the television, reflected off the lenses of her glasses.

"I am not all 'dolled-up,'" Murphy insisted, disliking, for whatever reason, the term.

"Where are you off to?" the snow-white haired old lady asked.

"I am going out."

"Out where?"

"Just OUT."

He did not want his grandmother, or anyone else, to know that he was going to the theater, because...If she told someone and that someone told another and then his, Murphy's friends, found out he went to the theater? Would they think him...weird? (Or maybe they would think no such thing. Maybe have no thoughts on the matter. In any case—and just in case—he did not want his theater-going publicly known.) He glanced at the TV. An actor whom he recognized, being interviewed by Merv Griffin. The actor's incandescent white-toothed smile plastered on his face and the TV screen.

"Where are the car keys?" Murphy asked, bending over the white hair and speaking in a low tone.

His brother stirred, turned onto his side and began to saw another log.

"What?" The old lady fiddled with her hearing aid. The aid squeaked. Squawked. She peered up at him. "What?" she said, evenly.

"Where are the car keys." Murphy enunciated clearly.

The old lady shook her head, wrinkles around her mouth tightening. "The Crosby's?" she asked. "They are not on until eight."

Murphy frowned. "The keys!" he said, making a turning motion with his hand. "Car keys!"

The old lady's smile faded. "What for?" she asked.

"To drive the car," Murphy said, 'what do think 'what for'?"

"How long do you need it?" she asked, querulously. "Your brother needs the car to go to work, you know."

Muphy side-glanced sleeping Al. "Yea, I know. Not long."

The old lady dug a wad of Kleenex, a chain of rosary beads, and the car keys from a pocket of her apron. "I hope I do not get in Dutch for this," she said, handing over the keys.

Murphy pulled the car to the curb in front of the Beckwith residence on Friend Street. The house a small peak-roofed two-story affair, like all the other houses lining the street.

He hit the car horn with the heel of his hand. He would not go to the door, he decided; too risky. Might meet Mr. and Mrs. Beckwith and get the third degree. He saw a shade move in a window. Good, he thought; the message of his coming would get to her, or maybe it was her at the window...He looked down at his suit, wondering if he had worn the right clothes. Was he overdressed? He wondered what would the people at the theater think of him? Maybe recognize him as some kind of writer and a good guy to know—an up and coming...whatever: prospect, like a good minor league ballplayer headed to the majors? He looked into the side mirror: most of his pimples had dried, he noted happily: the recent sunshine had done his face good.

"Who is that in the green car outside?" Mrs. Beckwith, standing at the living room window, asked. She scrutinized her daughter.

"Billy Murphy," Lucy Beckwith said. She glanced into the oval mirror hung on the wall. Spread the bangs of her short bobbed hair.

"Oh? The Murphy who went to school with your brother?" Mrs. Beckwith pulled the curtain aside.

Lucy rearranged her bangs. "Yes, mother—I told you he was taking me out."

"You did?" Mrs. Beckwith frowned. "Doesn't he know enough to come to the door?"

Lucy wet two fingers and pasted her bangs onto her forehead. "No," she said, "he does not know anything."

Should he beep the horn again, Murphy wondered. Would it be considered rude if he did? Some sort of unforgivable social faux pas? (And was 'faux pas' one word or two? And how was it spelled?) "Shit," he muttered, maybe he should forget the whole thing. Drive off, he told himself. Hell, it was her asked him to go. HER idea not his. And now to make him wait...Or was she waiting for him to come to the door? He looked to the house. She would be waiting a long time, he told himself. A goddamn long—

The front door of the house swung open. Murphy watched Lucy step from the door. She wore a knee-length sleeveless dress that looked, Murphy thought, like a smock that patients in hospitals wear. A lace thing, like a doily, around her neckline. The doily-thing made it seem as if her head were on a platter.

"Hi," she said, falling onto the front seat.

"Hi."

Murphy put the car in gear and drove, steering one-handed, other arm hung out the window and against the car door. Warm air of the twilit summer night tickled his face. "So, what is this play about?" he asked.

"It is called 'The Locker Room.' About a sports team in England that plays one of those games they play. One of those games with a ball."

"Rugby? Soccer?"

"Rugby, I think," she said tonelessly. She looked at a section of marshy swampland at the side of the road, cattails sticking up out the water. Who gives a shit, she thought, what kind of game?

A sports play, Murphy thought happily—maybe something like the play he had watched on television: 'Requiem for a Heavyweight.' Maybe this locker room play would give him an idea, he thought, for a play he would write, and then, who knows, get the theater to do it...Maybe meet someone at the theater, he told himself, who had some pull, somebody who could give him the scoop on the theater scene. He wondered what name he should put on the play (after he wrote it). Billy W. Murphy? William W. Murphy? W. W. Murphy?

"You ever see 'Requiem for a Heavyweight?" he asked.

"No," she said disinterestedly. "What is that?"

A sign in front of the Drive-In Movie Theater read: Inside Angela, staring Long John Silver XXX.

"It is a sports play. I saw it on TV. Anthony Quinn played the role of this boxer, a guy named 'Mountain" who wins all his fights and starts to think he is a great fighter but really all the fights are fixed. It was based on a true story—the life of Primo Carnera, a heavyweight giant who fought in, like, the nineteen-twenties..." He side-glanced Lucy. A red pimple on her shoulder the size of a dime. Why didn't she wear a dress with sleeves? Or put a band-aid on the splotch? He reached to the radio dial: the rich voice of Frank Sinatra came in loud and clear: "Strangers in the night, exchanging glances..."

W. William Murphy, he decided.

A flock of well-dressed and gaily chattering, so it seemed to Murphy, people, stood on the white marble steps below four fat Doric style columns fronting the theater. The people bathed in the soft blue and purple pastel twilight. The theater building between two of the many ivy and vine-coated prettified college buildings along the avenue.

Murphy stood alone, nervously unbuttoning and re-buttoning his suit coat. In no way, he had quickly realized, was he overdressed. A group of women on steps above him talked loudly and without apparent self-consciousness, one or another intermittently screeching with laughter. Fancy looking dames, some ancient, who wore enough jewelry between them to sink a canoe...No one gave, or had given him, so much as a glance, he noted; like he was invisible or something. He watched a raven-haired girl walk past on the arm of a tall slim guy with a pony-tail. He stared at the set of melons clearly outlined beneath the girl's silkily sheer dress. His breath caught in his throat. It was almost like she had nothing on! He cautioned himself against staring—it was bad manners, plus, if anyone saw him staring then that anyone might not speak to him, thinking he, Murphy, was some kind of dope or even crude bastard not worth talking to...Still, the girl was really something. The guy she was with looked, to Murphy, like a perfumed dope who probably had his hair cut at a beauty parlor.

Murphy checked the time by his watch, like a man in a hurry and with important things to do. He imagined someone coming up to him and asking how he was doing and he telling that someone—and he hoped it was her with the melons—that he was a writer and was thinking of doing a play, maybe have it shown at the theater if they, the theater people (whomever they were) liked it. Work in a reference to 'Requiem for a Heavyweight' so he would not seem like a bullshitter throwing the bull around but like someone who knew his stuff. He turned and smiled at a couple. The woman had sculpted hair and dark sunglasses, like, maybe, Murphy thought, she was some actress who did not want to be recognized and have people bug her for an autograph. The man had a hair-do also (maybe went to the same beauty parlor as the dopey guy) and was dressed completely in black, head to toe, with leather shoes on that Murphy bet cost a hell of a lot more than a few bucks. The guy's lips tightened in approximation of a smile. The woman did not move a muscle. Maybe she really was Gina Lolla-fucking-bridgida, Murphy thought. A guy behind the couple—thin straight-arrow guy with Marine Corp boot camp hair-cut, winked at Murphy. Murphy stared, caught off guard. The guy's lips spread in an unhealthy-looking smile. The guy did not look like any Marine Murphy had ever seen! He quickly turned his gaze. Jesus! He studied the outline of a weeping willow tree on the theater front lawn. He wondered if the fruit would try something. He pictured himself slamming a haymaker into the fruit's face. He turned to his right to face a guy with a tanned face the color of a raisin; around the guy's neck a handkerchief, tied, and on his face glasses with thick black rims. Hair slicked-back over his skull like he, the guy, had just come out of the shower. "Hey!" Murphy said exuberantly, "how you doin'?" The guy responded—after about three minutes—with a yawn. He ignored the hand Murphy thrust forward. Murphy waited for the guy to ask how he, Murphy, was doing, but the guy turned and slipped into the crowd. Murphy saw Lucy returning with the tickets. Compared to the raven-haired girl, and a few others Murphy had scooped-out, Lucy looked like a dog. He felt a little sorry for her, but she seemed oblivious to any difference between she and the others. He wondered how she had come to the decision to wear a goddamn hospital smock. The pimple on her shoulder looked big as a tomato.

"You want to go in?"

"Okay."

The theater seats were soft and comfortable, plush, like the place. Ritzy, like the inside of a high-priced casket, Murphy thought. Most of those around him seemed, to him, to be engaged in animated conversation. He wished that he too could have an animated conversation. He turned to a woman in the row behind but she looked right through him, as if he were glass. Half a dozen rows back sat the guy with the raisin-face. Murphy waved but the guy did not respond. A stiff, Murphy thought, who probably drank formaldehyde before coming to the theater...Maybe he should have drunk some too, he told himself. His theater experience was turning out to be a lot different than he had thought it would.

The place quickly filled. Looking around, Murphy realized that there were a lot of women—a ton of them, compared to the number of men. He wondered why. The overhead lights suddenly blinked on and off and the crowd hushed. The lights went off as the curtain rose

on a bare locker room, spartan, tall row of gray metal lockers and a bench parallel the lockers. Roar of crowd noise off-stage. Raucous noise of a vast crowd. From stage right the rugby players entered: disheveled, dirty, wounded lads in states of obvious exhaustion. About a dozen players. They threw themselves down on the bench and onto the floor. Behind them, a stout older man, wearing a sweat suit, pork pie cap, and whistle hung around his neck.

A realistic type play, Murphy thought happily. He hoped there would be at least one girl in it. Maybe one of the players has a girlfriend who will appear, he thought (but what would a girl be doing in a locker room?). He listened to the coach, the older man, speak with thick English accent.

Coach: (stage front) You have got to remember me laddies

When times is tough

You got to be rough

When you are getting beat under

Don't go asunder! Rise!

Get wise!

Give 'em the elbow and hip me lads!

Kick! Get slick, trip the

Bloody barstards…

Knee 'em in the jewels

Frig the friggin' rules

There is nothing wrong with cheating, lads

So long as you don't get caught!

Be sly, be wily; be fearless!

Remember Nelson on the quarter deck

Or the 400 in the valley–

Take off the diapers, boys!

Remember the Army at Wipers!

Gordon at Khartoum!

Kichener on the Nile!

The RAF above the channel

And bloody limees in Rangoon!

(coach punching fist into open hand)

Think of D-Day me lads

And the Royal Marines

Coming ashore on the bloody beach

Dodging bullets, throwing bloody

Bombs, blowing bloody Jerries

To hell and gone!

Scalin' the cliffs–

The tanks moving forward

Bloody fighters overhead…

(tall, well-built blonde-haired player, bare torso, leaps to
his feet, sings)

>Gordon at Khartoum!

>Kitchener on the Nile!

>The RAF above the channel

(other players join in on chorus)

>Bloody limees in Rangoon!

(another player, dark-haired, naked but for shorts)

>Never mind Calcutta

>And frig' the Cameroons

>We are the boys who won't be beaten

(chorus)

>Bloody limees in Rangoon!

(another player, red-head, fair freckled skin, sandy hair)

>Bugger all of Blighty

>From Peterlee to Portsmouth

>And Southend-on-the-Sea

>We are the lads who can't be beaten

>Saxons proud and free!

>Bugger Slim in Burma

>And Wolfe out in Quebec

>Bugger old Lord Nelson

>On the bloody quarterdeck!

>Bugger London and Pretoria

>And all the chaps between

>Bugger the Raj in New Delhi

>And the guns at El Alamein!

Muphy blinked and bolted upright in his seat. Two of the players, blonde and dark-hair, their bare asses turned to the audience and shining like full-moons. They were joined by others, all in jockstraps.

(players fling arms over each other's shoulders and begin a high-kick chorus line)

> We are the boys who can't be beaten
>
> The bloody limees in Rangoon
>
> The RAF above the channel
>
> And Gordon in Khartoum!

(players marching in place, fair-haired player out front)

Murphy stared, unbelieving, as the fair-haired guy out front ripped his jock strap off. His dick flip-flopped against this thighs as he approached stage front. Murphy side-glanced Lucy, sunk in her seat, her coal-black eyes riveted to the stage and, seemingly, glowing. The blonde and dark-haired player joined the fair-haired guy, all prancing around with their dorks hanging-out. Murphy looked about the theater. What were all the women looking at, he wondered: the play or the dicks? He sunk down in his seat. Deep, but not deep enough...

> Monty is in the desert–
>
> Winnie never quits
>
> We are the boys who can't be beaten–
>
> Douglas Haig is a piece of shit!
>
> Gordon at Khartoum
>
> Kitchener on the Nile
>
> The RAF above the channel
>
> And (audience members join in)
>
> Bloody limees in Rangoon!

(Coach, loud-calling)

Over the top me boys!

Tally ho and to the hunt!

We are off to Flanders Field

And to the bloody front!

Never mind the Maxim

Put mustard gas on ham

And use the bloody bayonet

On every bloody man!

(players doing a shuffling side-wards strut—dicks flopping)

Rhodes killed off the Matebele

Jamison attacked the Boers

Together they stole the gold and diamonds

To support the Brittish whores!

Cook is in Guiana

Gandi's in the clink

The Union Jack is rising

Swim lads or we will bloody well sink!

(chorus of marchers)

Bloody well sink!

Bloody well sink!

(coach)

Remember Dunkirk me lads

Remember Singapore

Hong Kong and Malaya!

The REPULSE and the PRINCE OF WALES

Did not sail for nothing my boys

Nor did old Blighty

Catch the blitz

For the fun of it!

The V-2 could not put us under

You know the reason why?

Remember the bridge over the River Kwai?

Remember Bomber Harris?

The goose-steppers did not scare us...

The voices of the actors became a distant babble to Murphy. He told himself get up and go, leave, walk-out! He glanced back, up the aisle. A long walk to the EXIT sign. Everyone would stare at him were he to walk; maybe even the actors would see him leave, and their feelings be hurt...He did not have the guts. He squirmed in the suddenly uncomfortable seat as the play went on. He thought of all the women in the joint: come to see the strip-show, only they, the women, would probably call it "art" (and call a strip-show "smut").

At the end of the act he stood and walked out to the lobby. Sat in a plush chair and chit-chatted with the ticket-taker, a middle-aged man who regarded Murphy with slight amusement. Murphy did not tell the guy that he, Murphy, was a writer or that he was interested in producing a play.

Murphy drove, both hands on the steering wheel.

"Nah, I am kind of tired," he said, rubbing a hand over his face. "Long day, you know? And I have to get up early tomorrow." He glanced to a roadside FRIENDLY'S restaurant, the place luminous, like a full moon in a haze. He punched the accelerator and the Chevy shot past three cars on the straight-away.

"Oh come on!" Lucy whined. "I do not want to go home now."

"I can't," he said coldly.

"We could stop for just a half-hour," Lucy said, hopefully.

"Nah..." Who gives a fuck what you want, Murphy thought, expertly wheeling the car around the corner and onto Friend Street. Golden windows of houses like nightlights guiding Murphy through the dark.

"You are no fun," Lucy said sullenly, pouting.

"Yea, well, like I said..."

Murphy brought the car to an abrupt halt in front of the Beckwith residence. "See you later," he barked.

Lucy exhaled an "oh!" and stepped from the car, slamming the door shut as if trying to break it, the car or door. She watched the son of a bitch drive away. She hoped he got into an accident. She turned and trudged toward her house. Scenes from the play ran through her mind: the lithe white bodies of the actors she had studied in detail. The bodies moved step for step with her down the walkway. She felt heat between her legs: reaching beneath her dress, she touched the dampness of her underwear. Images of the players filtered through her mind... The heat spread from her crotch to her thighs and into her belly. She ran her hands over her small pert breasts: her nipples tingled as if electrified.

She saw a man's body sprawled over the porch before the front door of the house. She peered at the form.

Grimacing, Lucy prodded the inert body with the toe of her loafer. "Dad!" she said, savagely. "Wake up!" She kicked him in the ribs.

The man groaned, waking. "Wha'?" he muttered. "Wha'?" Raising himself onto his elbows, he peered about. Lucy looked to the road. Thought, what if someone, at this moment, came to visit? What if one of her friends or relatives suddenly pulled up into the driveway? She watched disgustedly as her father struggled to his knees, then, with hands flat on the floor, straighten his legs. Were any of the neighbors looking out of their windows, Lucy wondered. She looked up at the dark windows of the Larson's house next door. Mr. Beckwith tipped, wedging his head and shoulders against the door, his rear end raised in the air. He clawed his way up the face of the door to a standing position. A thin knotted-up little man, he swayed, doing a wobbly two-step, and fell against Lucy as she tried to squeeze past him. The flagrant smell of booze wafted into her face as her father's stringently muscled body pressed up against her. He moaned and flung his arms around her shoulders. Lucy hugged him to her. Finding his mouth, she thrust her tongue deep into the old man's throat.

The front door swung open as the overhead light illuminated the porch. Mrs. Beckwith stood in the doorway: "what in the world is going on here?" she demanded.

Buddies

A foggy morning in the orange grove in Thonotosassa, Florida, the sun broiling the horizon, baking the world. A farmer wearing slouch-hat, suspenders, rubber boots, strolling through the wet grass, hands in overall pockets: "You boys can have this row here," he says, accent making 'here' sound like 'haere.' He nods to trees the size of small houses, row upon row, more appearing by the minute as the sun vaporizes the fog.

I do not like being called 'boy'–I am twenty-one years old and a man. A man ready to do a man's work for man-sized pay.

"Picking oranges?" the black clerk at the store where we bought beer the day before had asked. "That be a man's work." The clerk had a smooth round face and a body soft-looking as a baby. He wore a dress shirt and slacks; belt bisecting his egg-shaped torso. He reminded me of my grandfather—he was my grandfather; everyone's grandfather.

Leno, Louie, and I had squatted against the outside wall of the store while we ate baloney sandwiches and drank beer.

"Man, is it frickin' hot," Louie complained, wiping his face with a red bandanna he wore on his head like a kerchief. His small black eyes glittered; his big sun-burnt nose shaped like the prow of a ship.

Leno had sprawled on the walkway, long legs stretched; he had poked a finger into a hole and extracted a two-inch long beetle. "Look," he had said excitedly. He held the beetle up to his coke bottle thick glasses. "A Rhinoceros beetle! I never see one this—ow!" He dropped the beetle onto the pavement; it hit with the heft of a golf ball. Leno, on all fours, continued to scrutinize the bug. "These things can grow to six inches in the jungle," he had said, "they live on figs. I read an article in 'Scientific American' about them..." He picked the beetle up. "They can really pinch," he added.

"Wonder how hot it will get today?" Louie had said. "A hundred?" He upended a can of beer and had guzzled; I had watched his Adam's apple bob...

With the fog lifting, we drop the oranges one by one to the earth, tunk tunk thump

tump

    thunk

       tunktunktunk

thump

    tunktunk

    thunk. Question: how many oranges does it take to fill a three foot deep by five foot wide bin? Answer: a shit-load. And one shit-load equals five dollars. Six loads, thirty dollars. Ten bucks a day for each of us.

The farmer is friendly; he lets us sleep in his tent in the grove. The floor of the tent is dirt. A whip-poor-will whistles nightly its plaintive mournful call. One night I wake to the sound of something trying to claw its way through the tent. I elbow Leno who sputters awake; he screams, I scream: the clawing ceases and the creature, whatever it was, gone; the night quiet for a second before the insects begin again their ungodly screeching.

Orange juice for breakfast, orange pulp for lunch and dinner; oranges on the side and for dessert. Goddamn oranges! They cling to the tree branches like frightened children to their mothers. The thorns of the branches rip flesh. Wearing long-sleeve shirts saves flesh but the shirts quickly become sopped with sweat. The bins fill slower than a baseball game. Eight bins one day, best we could do. Not nearly as good as the Jamaicans in the next row; friendly people but remote, too busy to chat or maybe too afraid. They work on Saturday and so do we. The farmer comes by late in the morning, atop his tractor. "Working on a Saturday (Satt-day), hey?" he exclaims. "Pretty soon you boys be getting kinky hair!"

Sunday we go for a swim at the locale waterhole, a dismal rocky stretch of "beach" below and to the side of a highway overpass. The water of the quick flowing river cool, dark, and green. Everyone on the beach has a least half-a-bag on, some passed-out and lying like logs. A stench of oil and fuel wafts down from the overpass. Trucks belch black exhaust clouds. A gang of kids tries to pull a bathing suit off a woman lying in the sand. She struggles mightily against the little rats to save her modesty.

The water is like manna from heaven. I stand in line on the bank waiting to swing out over the river on the end of a rope fastened high in a tree. I ask the guy in front of me if there are alligators in the river. He has long straggly hair and a chisel-shaped face. "Around the bend," he says, pointing.

I float down around the bend: it looks darker than up-river: a thick wall of green trees and shrubs rising from the bank. I drift with the current. Suddenly feel something touch my foot. I pull my legs up and reverse direction, swimming like Johnny Weissmuller, and sweating by the time I reach the beach. Louie and Leno wiggle around in the water like puppies.

We give the straggly-haired chisel-faced guy a ride to his trailer. I ask him if he knows where we can find some magic mushrooms (psilocybin). He says there are some in the meadow behind his trailer. Says the farmer who owns the land might take a pot shot at us if we wander through; says that if we hear a rattle, better get out and away.

The trailer park grass is rusty-colored. Louie can't climb the wire fence because of his bum leg. Leno and I walk around the meadow. Do not hear any rattles but do see some spiders big as dinner plates. Leno almost walks face-first into one fixed onto a web. Do not see any mushrooms, not the white ones with a colorful ring around the stem, or any other kind. After some nerve-wracking minutes, listening for a rattle and watching for a farmer with a gun, we leave.

On our way back to the grove, Louie says, "we got to get this car fixed. You hear that thumping noise? You think it is coming from the engine?" Sweat beads his face. The car—a black Volkswagen Beetle—bakes, air from the open window like a hair dryer pointed at my face.

"Stop being paranoid," Leno says.

"I am not paranoid, Leno!" Louie glares into the rear view mirror. "What do you care, anyway?" he asks, "it is not your car."

On Monday the farmer arrives in our row, riding his motorized chariot. Says he has some news to pass on. Louie is standing on a ladder; I on a tree limb; Leno holds a twelve foot-long pole that has a rope noose on the end (used to rip the topmost oranges from the trees). The farmer says that his daughter, who is working elsewhere in the grove, has got the eye for us and we should take care because, if she nabs us, we will go straight to hell (haell) in a hurry, as she is "that kind of gal." He drives off, grinning. In the afternoon we glimpse the girl, a pig-tailed blonde wearing blue jeans, standing on a ladder in a tree some distance off. It takes us longer than usual to fill the next bin. Eager to go to hell, we take a long gander. The work slows to a standstill. Louie barks, "come on you guys! Pick some oranges—get busy!"

"Don't sweat the small stuff," Leno says laconically.

"Fuck you, Leno," Louie says. "You want to stay here for the rest of your life? Is that what you want—pick oranges for the rest of your life? Hanh? Well, I don't!"

"OK Coach," I say.

"Fuck you too Kell," Louie says sourly. "Christ, how did I get stuck with you two for friends anyway?"

Late in the afternoon, Leno goes on strike, refusing to work at all. Lies in the shade on a blanket and picks at a quarter-sized scab on his chest, where a cyst used to be before he operated on himself with a jackknife.

At dusk, we go to the store, buy beer and a bottle of brandy. It is agreed that, on Friday, we split and head to the coast.

Around the campfire, we exhaust the subject of the farmer's daughter and become mute. The fire crackles, the insects scream. Leno's eyes glow coal red. Louie sits with a blanket over his head, poncho-style. His sunken eyes look like puddles about to run down his cheeks. Empty beer cans, at his feet, glimmer in the fire light. "I don't know why you guys let me hang around with you," he says, maudlin. "You don't even like me. I know you don't."

"Oh for chrissakes," Leno says disgustedly.

"It is true," Louie insists. "I know you don't."

"I like you," Leno says tonelessly.

"Me too," I say.

"Fuck you guys!" Louie barks.

"Stop feeling sorry for yourself," Leno advises.

"Why shouldn't I feel sorry for myself, Leno? You ever have a mobile home fall on top of you? You ever get your pelvis crushed? NO! You didn't! Well, I did! 'You will never walk again,' that is what they told me in the hospital. Be in a wheelchair for life. HA!"

Louie pulls his right work boot off; a steel orthopedic brace, attached to the boot, glimmers in the fire light. He tosses the boot onto the campfire. "I don't need a brace," he announces, standing, shedding the poncho. "I can walk as good as any man!" he shouts. He stumbles in a half-circle, the calf of his right leg thin like a fleshy Popsicle stick. "ANY MAN ALIVE!"

Leno digs the boot out of the fire.

Louie falls, plops onto the dirt on his seat, pulls the blanket around his shoulders.

Weeeeeeeeeeeeeep! The insects screech.

Weeeeeeeeeeeeeep!

Weeeeeeeeeeeeeep!

Friday morning: Louie drives, Leno and I stand on the back bumper of the car and ride it like bronco busters, whooping and laughing as the car bounces over the ruts and moguls of the dirt road.

We stop at a bar along the roadside. Soft yellow light inside; we order a frosty golden pitcher of beer and three cigars and sit at a table and smoke and drink like men of opulence. Lacking money for a second pitcher, we leave, drive to a garage, and buy a tire for the car, then we head northeast toward the coast and Daytona Beach. Leno lies across the backseat, bare feet out the car window. I find a roach, left from the bag of

Columbian Gold we started the trip with, under the mat, and light up. Louie and I get a few good tokes. The sweat on my body instantly dries. The car floats over the road. Louie looks serene, red bandanna rolled and tied around his head. He glances at me, smiles; one of his capped front teeth is chipped, like someone took a nail and gouged a hole. "What did you say?" he asks. The flat paisley green landscape goes past the car windows. The car engine hums. I turn the radio on and Beethoven's Fifth Symphony begins—the violin notes, after the initial don-don-don-tah, run up and down my spine. Louie reaches and changes the station: "I hate that crap," he says.

Barry Manilow sings, "Lola, she was a showgirl, at the Copa, Copa Cabana."

Louie pulls off the highway and into the lot of a seven/11 store. He forks a few of our few remaining dollars out for a six-pack of beer. The black girl running the cash register tells me that I am "cute." "Him?" Louie says, "you must be blind."

The first swallow of beer is like letting a mountain stream run down my throat. Louie guzzles the stuff like a man dying of thirst. Leno lays back, a beer balanced on his flat tanned stomach, a copy of 'Scientific American' magazine in his hands. I reach into the glove box for the book I have been reading since Tennessee: The Bold Saboteurs by Chandler Brossard.

Waves flop onto shore over the top of a white jellyfish. Leno pokes the thing with a stick and then, bare-handed, turns the jellified mass over. A small kid says "those things sting." Leno picks the thing up. A towel-sized gob like a hunk of calcified spit. He brings the creature to within a few inches of his glasses and gives it the once-over. "You are going to get stung, Leno," Louie says. Leno turns and holds the fish out to a girl. She screams and runs off. "You dummy," Louie says, "she was nice—maybe we could have picked her up." Leno hawks a loogie into the sand. "Pick that up," he says.

The heat smothers the beach in a bear hug. Leno digs himself into the sand like a hedgehog. Louie lies like a mummy as he bakes. I go for a walk up the beach. A girl in a bikini, lying at the water's edge, says, "hey, muscles!"

I keep walking. Embarrassed. Up to the pier where a fisherman has hooked a giant sea turtle that rises out of the water, encased in its great fortress-shell. The sight thrills me. The fishing line snaps and the turtle sinks. I am glad. I walk back to the beach and enter the water, swim out a good distance and stand on a sand bar, water to my waist. People on the beach look tiny: I try and focus in on the girl who said hello to me. Why did I not say something to her? Stop and chat...I wonder if there are sharks nearby in the murky gray-green water...A well-built strawberry-blonde.

I hear a whistle and see a lifeguard running around the beach like he is going to a fire. Whistling at me, I realize. I start the trek back to shore.

Leno and Louie stand by the car; Louie holds a scrap of paper in his hand. "Some guy," he says, "told us where to find mushrooms. All's we have to do is go to this bar and find 'Harry.'"

After leaving the beach we find the bar but not Harry.

On return to the rest area, it starts to pour rain. Lightning bolts flicker out of the gray murk of storm. Rain drops the size of grapes crush themselves against the windshield. Leno says that a lot of lightning comes up from the ground not from the sky. Louie says, "my ass it does." Leno begins an explanation of electrical conduction properties. Louie interrupts: "Leno, how can you be so smart and so fucking goofy at the same time?"

During our dinner of baloney sandwiches washed down with water from the rest area fountain, we discuss finances.

It is agreed that in the morning we will look for jobs.

Each of us picks a picnic table to sleep on. I fall asleep to the sound of cars and trucks sloughing along the nearby Interstate. I dream of picking oranges: filling bins twenty feet high and deep. The grove on an island in the middle of an ocean. A boat arrives from the sea: on board are Louie and President Jimmy Carter. "You have done enough," the President says to me. "Your country is proud of you." He hands me a gold medal shaped like a peanut. Behind him, on the horizon, a giant mushroom-shaped cloud has formed.

A non-stop procession of shiny chrome automobiles and belching trucks on the Interstate.

Louie sits slump-shouldered atop a picnic table.

"I do not want to work for MCDONALD'S," I say.

"Tough shit! You think I do? You think he does?" Louie looks down at Leno sprawled in the shade beneath the table. "Christ, Kell, we got a tank of gas and five bucks between us."

Leno flips a page of the textbook he is reading: The World of Microbiology.

I feel foolish and conspicuous in my paisley blue and yellow-striped MCDONALD'S shirt. I tell myself I will wear the shirt—I have to—but not the goofy white-peaked paper hat.

Leno is given grill duty, flipping burgers; Louie is bun-man, in charge of condiments; I am trash-man and work outside on the basketball court-sized patio.

I stuff the cap into my pocket and for the first few hours busy myself cleaning and emptying and replacing trash bags. Then I sit, out of sight of anyone looking out the window of the building. Other people sit around me, including lots of street people, all of whom have stories. Some of them heavy raps, most not. I get up now and then and walk by the window so the manager gets an occasional glimpse of me. When I go inside for more bags, the manager—balding, with a comb-over, and constipated look—tells me

"button your shirt," and asks where my cap is.

Leno talks to the customers as he works—shouts from the grill behind the counter. He tells the manager "don't sweat the small stuff, Bugsy." Louie has a harried look; he is struggling to keep the condiments straight.

At shift's end we steal a box of quarter-pounder's from the freezer. We press the meat into log rolls around a stick, and toast the rolls over a fire, like meatloaf on a stick. The fire crackles, embers glow. A raucous chorus of crickets grows louder in the fading light.

In the morning, a blazing yellow sun. We drive to the beach. The merciless sun inescapable except in the thin slice of shadow the car casts.

We say hello to girls. Louie talks two into sitting in the car with he and I. I become tongue-tied, nearly mute, sitting next to a girl with a spare-tire around her middle but large breasts and smooth manilla skin, and wearing a bikini bottom the size of a washcloth. Louie has to carry the conversation with both. It does not last long before they leave.

Our second night at MCDONALD'S a new manager replaces the former. Halfway through the shift the guy asks Louie: "who is that guy with the MCDONALD'S shirt on in the courtyard?"

Piles of plates, napkins, and wrappers overflow the trash containers. I am sitting with my feet up on a bench when the manager taps me on the shoulder. "You're fired," he says.

I walk out to the parking lot. Leno lies, sprawled across the sidewalk, his head resting on the curb. People have to step over him to walk past. He chews on a MCDONALD'S straw as he stares up at the full-moon in a sea-blue sky.

"I got fired," I say.

"So did I. That new manager did not like me calling him 'Bugsy.'"

"You know," Leno says, "for a long time people thought that the moon came out of the earth—from the Pacific Basin region. It wasn't until Apollo 11 brought those rocks back, and the rocks were analyzed, that they realized the moon had a different origin than they thought, see? They knew some kind of collision had to have occurred, just after the earth was formed, see, 4.5 billion years ago. They think another planet, about the size of Mercury, slammed into earth and the debris from the collision got caught up in the gravitational pull of earth and the moon formed...Pretty neat, huh?"

"Yeah."

MCDONALD'S wrappers, bags, napkins, flop and slither up and down the street as the wind blows.

Louie approaches across the lot. "I just quit," he says. "They offered me a management-trainee position to keep me, but I said 'no.'" He looks around the lot and street; turns his big nose up. "Fuck MCDONALD'S," he says.

A fat man stands on a railroad sliding, a line of rusty brown box cars behind him. "You the boys from MANPOWER?" he asks. "Yep," Leno says. The neck-less turnip-shaped fat man has a small head. "Park over there," he says, "next to that building. There is one of you already here."

I step from the car. Dust floats around my feet. Squint in the over-bright sunlight. Weeds around the sliding and tracks. Burnt brown grass and white bleached rocks in a dusty field. Like the place was abandoned after being bombed.

"This here is—what was your name?" The fat men reaches a hand to a guy standing in a box car. "Red," the guy says. "This here is Red; I explained everything to him. He will tell you what to do."

Bags of cement mix, stacked six feet high, fill the car. Sunlight through the car door lights dust particles swarming the air, glinting mica specks shining bright against the brown background of the car. Red has long strawberry-blonde Jesus hair and green eyes. He is thin but wiry. "These bags (bag-ags)," he says, "have to be stacked on pallets so's the fork lift can take them out."

"Holy Christ," Louie says. "That is a lot of bags. How much they weigh?"

"Hunnert pounds each."

We work as teams. It is hard for me to breath in the dusty air; hard to keep sweat out of my eyes. I can see the pain on Louie's face whenever he twists his foot wrong. After an hour of work, I suggest a break. Louie snarls: "don't think I can take it, do you? You are going to treat me like a pussy, right? Well, I don't need a break! FUCK YOU. You take a break!"

"Take it easy, Crip," Leno says.

"Don't call me 'Crip' Leno," Louie says.

At noon we drive to the seven/11 store, buy baloney and bread. Red is broke so we share our lunch. He tells us stories of his travels, hitch hiking tales on highways across the country. Drug stories too, of the times he took peyote, opium, mescaline, and 'schrooms and the particular high each induced.

The day grows longer, the sun hotter, the bags heavier.

The fat man returns, says, "you boys is good workers." Leno, Louie, and me go to the office and pick up checks then to a bank. The teller says the bank charges two dollars to cash checks for people without an account. Leno demands to speak to the manager. The manager, in suit and tie, looks like Howard from the old Andy Griffith TV show. "Look Bugsy," Leno says, "this is illegal! I will go to the Board of Labor and report you! I will go to the Attorney General's office! You can't do this—it is bullshit!" Leno slams his fist down on the desktop. "I will go to Jimmy Carter!!"

Howard, face red, says that either we leave immediately or he calls the police.

We leave and go into the bank next door. They charge us three dollars per check.

With our checks plus MCDONALD'S money, we are flush. Fat City. We hit the bars and the night soon becomes hilarious. The beer goes down smooth. Somewhere along the way we decide to drink shots. A bad decision, for me; I lose my mind, lose Leno and Louie, black-out, and come-to, in daylight, the sun pouring acid on my face as I lie, on my back, twenty feet above the beach on a wooden platform resembling an umbrella. One of half-a-dozen platforms along the beach. How I climbed onto the roof of the thing is a mystery, to me. My shoulder hangs off the edge and I am missing my shirt. I avoided cops but, holy shit, if I had fallen off of the floor?

I stagger around the streets until I find the car. Leno and Louie passed-out in the front seats.

"Hey, wake up!"

Leno stirs.

"We have to go to work."

Leno's eyes like knife-slits. "Work?"

"Yeah, MANPLOWER."

We stop at a seven/11. I buy a cold can of V-8 juice and guzzle it (my hangover cure).

Our job of the day is working with a guy from up North who installs refrigerator units. He likes us—mainly because we too from the North—and treats us to a lunch of hush puppies and fried chicken. After work we drive to the bar to look for Harry and the 'schrooms.

A crowded red-neck bar in the middle of a big gravel lot. I win three games on the bar's pool table; enough to keep us in beer for the night. I choke on a shot at the 8-ball in a fourth game, and go to the bar for a mixed drink as the beer is tasting bitter to me. The jukebox plays 'Sweet Home Alabama.' I ask the bartender for quarters to play the jukebox.

"Good shooting," a guy at the bar says. Thought that 8-ball was going in."

"So did I."

The guy wears glasses and a Boston Red Sox ball cap. "Where you from?" he asks.

"Massachusetts."

"So am I. Brockton, Mass."

"Rocky Marciano!"

"Yeah! The Marciano's lived two streets over from the house where I grew up." The guy holds out his hand. "Name is Harry." His hand is dry and warm.

"Harry? Hey—we have been looking for you, man. No shit!"

Harry blinks. "You don't work for the Federal Bureau of Narcotics do you? Or the Volusia County PD?"

"No! Christ, we work for MANPOWER."

"That the place that takes half your pay?"

"Yea, a slavery racket. Hey, come and meet my friends."

I usher Harry to our table. Leno and Louie say howdy. We shoot the shit for awhile before the subject turns to 'schrooms. Harry agrees to take us to the 'schrooms.

We get into the car, drive down dirt roads until Harry tells us to stop. He leads the way into the meadow. We stop when he stops. Follow the angle of his pointed finger leading to a little grove of white mushrooms, colorful rings around their stems. We fill a shopping bag full, return to the car, and drive to Harry's trailer.

Harry packs the mushrooms into a wire colander and suspends the colander over water boiling in a pot. We drink beer and chat while the "tea" is brewing. Harry hands out 16-ounce glasses of brackish green liquid. Stuff that tastes nothing like mushroom soup.

At the trailer door, Harry wishes us a good trip. Leno drives the car, I ride shotgun. We have been had, I think; nothing is happening. I feel no different. I look at Leno; we are stopped at a red light. He has a sort of slant to his eyes, like an Asiatic person. The car engine races and the car seems to rise, snort, and wiggle a little on its rubber feet. Leno laughs an un-healthy-sounding laugh. I wonder what he is laughing about. I hear the voice on the radio announce that an important mes-sage is forthcoming. I listen intently. Hear a burp followed by a gushing sound. I look back: Louie holds the Styofoam cooler in his hands. "I puked!" he says. "Now what do I do?"

Louie looks strangely hairier to me. Early genus of caveman. "You've ruined your high."

"I know," he says frantically. "What do I do?"

The car bucks forward, engine whining. The vomitus sloshes around in the cooler.

"YE-Hah!" Leno shouts.

"I am going to drink it." Louie raises the cooler to his lips.

"Cool it, Leno," I say. He is acting strange—I wonder what his problem is. He shushes me. "Listen!" He tilts his head toward the radio. We both listen—another important announcement.

A new car wash opening in Daytona Beach.

"Hey! You guys!" Louie wipes his mouth with the back of his hand. "Don't ever tell anyone about this, OK? About what I just done?"

The car seems to bend on the turns, as if made of some elastic material instead of metal. Streaks of multi-colored lights flash from passing car headlights and road signs.

"Where are we going?" Louie asks.

"I don't know," Leno says. "Why?"

"Go straight," I advise.

"We are being followed," Louie says.

Two huge yellow lights behind us, just off the back bumper. Like evil eyes. It is some kind of...spaceship? A steel wall rises on our left as the truck roars past, noise of its engine like a signal for Armageddon. A blast of a horn like the grunt of a stricken beast.

"What do you mean, Leno, 'I don't know.'" Louie insists.

"What does it matter?" Leno shrugs. "One way is the same as any other."

"It matters to me!" Louie shouts. His head hangs between the bucket seats. "You should have taken a left back there. This is the road to...nowhere!"

The car bends a shoulder into a curve. "Nowhere is the same as somewhere," Leno states. "It is all relative."

"My ass," Louie says. "Take this left up here."

The car grunts in protest on the turn. Warm velvety air of the night massages my face like soft fuzzy animals rubbing themselves against me. "Leno," I ask, "do you have relatives in Asia?"

"I told you," he says, "it is all relative."

"Hey," Louie says, his head back between the seat. "What are you guys talking about? About me, right? You are going to tell everybody about what I done, right?"

The rest area appears like a mirage in a desert. It is like a miracle, I think; our arrival. Like some invisible presence guided us...The earth beneath my boots is soft and somehow welcoming. The grass looks like a Persian carpet; I get a strong sense of the grass, the earth, inviting me to sit. The grass likes me. "Hey hey hey," the insects chant percussively, like the rhythm section of a conga band. A half-moon beams; an act, it seems to me, of pure generosity. An act of love. The moon loves us. Loves me...Stars send a radiant luster; a pure radiance—beyond beauty, I think. The stars are alive, it occurs to me. Everything is alive! The universe, like us, like me, breaths in & out, in & out...

Louie hands me a bottle of beer. The beer slides down my throat like a delicious nectar.

"You know what?" Louie says, eyes sparkling like diamonds in a face of onyx, "there are no two guys I would rather be with than you two. Let's be friends forever. Okay? Okay, Leno? Okay, Kell? Okay?"

Attaboy in the Sixth

He limped down the thin gravel driveway to the mailbox at the edge of the lawn. The latch on the opening of the mailbox stuck; he tore the goddamn latch open, reached, shuffled half a dozen envelopes, and shoved one into his dungaree jacket pocket. He limped up the street along the sidewalk, opposite Goldman's Supermarket. Gray sky above thick as pea soup. Purple ridge line of mountains below charcoal sky. Get a move on, he told himself, before the rain comes.

At the corner, he glanced across the intersection at the brown brick paper mill, a dark-eyed, three story oblong box. A woman wheeled a baby carriage alongside the mill. The baby stared, button eyes opened wide. He hustled across at the light, his bum leg aching below the knee, above the clasp of the metal orthopedic brace he wore. The digital clock, like an up-turned fly-swatter in front of the bank, read 11:38. He swung the gleaming glass door open and entered the glossy, polished interior. A teller turned a pear-shaped face and even, white teeth his way. The mouth smiled, corners of the lips arching upward. "Hiya," he said, slipping his check across the counter. The girl glanced at the check. "Signature, please." She rolled a pen along the counter. He put his John Hancock down: Louie L. Lipkin. The girl counted out his money. Louie stared at the girl's chest; she did not have much to look at. He glanced at the bank vault: thick metal door hanging from hinges and a metal wheel with spokes, like the wheel of a clipper ship, sprouting bug-like from the door's center. He saw himself sticking-up the place ("Alright, this is a stick-up!"), waving a pistol, and running out of the joint with a bag of loot. It'd take guts, he reflected, more guts than he had or ever would have. Guts like you read about. "Thank you," the girl sing-songed, pushing bills across the counter. "Thanks, Schweetheart," Louie said to the smile. The girl turned away, not hearing his Bogart impersonation, or else choosing to ignore him; probably the latter, he told himself.

He stood at the side of the street waiting for a car to let him cross. Watched the cars. Run their own mothers over, he thought. Run Jesus over and the Pope, too. "Try some oil," he shouted at a rattling orange dump truck belching smoke. DRINK 7-UP, the side panel of a delivery truck read. "OK, I will," Louie said, watching a shiny white Cadillac driven by a pouty-faced, red-lipped blonde. Was the rig the blonde's? he wondered. Probably belonged to some guy with big bucks, he'd bet. A Sugardaddy—an old prune-faced bastard who bought broads like he, Louie, bought loafs of bread. He crossed the street, wondering if life would be easier if he were a girl. He walked down an alleyway to a set of railroad tracks and walked the tracks behind a row of brick and clapboarded buildings.

Wave your hand and guys throw money at you, was that what it was like for them? He stepped over the ties. The doll in the Caddy would not wait long before some guy bought her a drink, he knew that. Stepping up onto cement sliding, he limped through the open back door of DD's Bar & Grill.

Three men sat at one end of the dark bar. The men swiveled their heads toward Louie and back again in one quick, unified motion. Louie squinted toward the bald-headed, husky bartender. "What is this," Louie complained, "a fucking morgue?"

"Hey, Sure-Shot," the bartender, wearing a clean white shirt, said unenthusiastically. Louie arranged himself on a stool at the bar end furthest the three guys. "How goes it?" the bartender asked, putting aside his racing form. Louie's grunt encapsulated his thoughts on life. The bartender scrupulously drew a draft beer. "Gimme a little guy, too, Petey." Louie laid a ten-spot on the bar. Petey dribbled whiskey into a glass. Louie drank the shot like a man dying of thirst. The taste gagged him; he took a swallow of beer. The beer was good. It hit the spot.

Petey leaned back against the cash register, a White owl cigar in his mouth. He puffed out five smoke rings. The rings wobbled in air before drifting together to form the Olympic logo.

Louie reached for the SPRINGFIELD REPUBLICAN newspaper on the bar and turned the pages to RED SOX. Coming off of spring training. Yaz could be tough this year, he thought. Maybe another '67. That'd be something! Maybe get tickets to a game, he told himself (even though the city bastards soaked you for all you were worth). MURDER in Springfield. Stabbed twelve times. Mad Dog Killer in custody. Two guys fighting over a broad. He wondered what the woman looked like, wished the paper had run a picture of her. He spent twelve minutes reading the story. The Mad Dog Killer stared from a black & white mug shot: black pupils in white orbs, thick nose and lips, bushy Afro, bull neck...Not a guy he wanted to meet in a dark alley (or a brightly lit one). CHILD ABUSE in Pittsfield. What could possess a man? Louie wondered. He did not recognize the name of the accused. Some dirty son of a TAXES going up again, of course; good old Taxachusetts, government had everybody by the short hairs.

He looked up at his reflection in the mirror, narrowed his eyes to slits like a tough guy who could stare holes through sheet metal.

A red-head at the bar end brayed a laugh. Like a goddamn hyena. Louie listened to the guy's blather. About how he liked his job hauling sheet rock. If carrottop liked his job so much, how come he wasn't working? Probably a sloucher, Louie decided; probably carried five sheets a day then shot his mouth off about it. The other two wore green gas station uniforms, names over the pockets. One told Red how hard he ("Pinky") worked in the gas station. The other gas station guy ("Al") scoffed: "Why, you don't do shit," he said. Louie laughed. The telephone beside the cash register squawked. Petey picked up the receiver. Louie plucked a quarter off the bar, stepped down onto the newly-mopped, paper-thin, brown linoleum. "ATTABOY in the sixth," Petey said, "three to one."

Louie slid the quarter into the Wurlitzer, pressed two buttons. The smooth notes of Boots Randolph's saxophone flowed from the machine like good booze down Louie's throat. He looked out the picture window. Sparrows flew from telephone lines. A white and green laundry truck scooted around the street corner. An old man shuffled along the walk before a brown tenement building. The paint on the tenement was peeled and flaked, like someone had tried to scrape the house using their fingernails. Would he ever be an old geezer with one foot in the grave? And how would he feel, he wondered, so close to kicking the bucket? A red Mustang passed. Girl driving looked like Iris. Iris! He wondered if Iris was still on the pill. Jesus, he hoped so! But if she wasn't and popped a kid out? Say it wasn't his. But what if the kid had the snoz, the big Lipkin beak? Be a dead giveaway. A cold sweat crept over his forehead; he took breaths, in...out...in...out. Iris was no dummy, he told himself; she knew enough to take care of herself. Or did she? Maybe she wanted to get knocked-up! Thought he'd marry her if she had one in the oven. Too bad for her if she thought so, he told himself. He could not see getting hitched to anyone, certainly not to a divorcee with two kids, each by a different husband. "Shit," he muttered, walking back to the bar.

"Petey!"

Louie watched the foam rise in the glass as Petey poured. The foam was like his life, rising to the surface only to evaporate like a promise unfulfilled, all bubbles and air. Louie smiled, surprised such a comparison had come to his mind. Like poetry it was. And was it true, too? And if so, what could he do about it? Get married? Would it be foolish to settle down (at his age, twenty-six?), buy a house (on what, his looks or hers?), have a kid or two (he could do that)...Iris was not a bad girl—a little wild and she liked her sauce, but who doesn't?

"That's right," Petey said into the telephone, "BABY TIME in the 5th, two to one; TRAMP A'HOY in the 8th, no odds."

Louie gulped his beer. Baby Time? What kind of name was that for a horse? He pinched a dime off the bar, walked to the telephone on the wall and dialed.

"Yea!" Louie said. "Whatayadoin'?" (BWWWWaaaaaa! One of Iris's kids bawled).

"Nothin'," Iris said, chewing gum.

Splack. Splick.

"What do you mean, nothin'?" Louie asked like an accusation.

"Wait a minute." KUMP, the receiver hit the countertop; Iris screamed, "shut-up!"

"Hello?"

"Yea," Louie said.

"I got something to tell you but not over the phone."

"Huh? Like what?" Louie asked, irritated.

"I don't want to over the phone," Iris whined girlishly.

"C'mon, Iris," Louie urged, "spill the beans! What is it?"

"Well..." Splick. "I..." Scquipp. "Missed my period."

"Your first one?"

"No, my second."

Pock.

"Iris, I will talk to you later." Louie hung up and walked wooden-leggedly back to the bar. Jesus goddamn Christ. His legs felt stiff and bis bum leg still ached. He dropped onto his bar stool. It never did rain either, he realized, looking out the bar window.

The Saboteurs

"Why do you sit like that?" she asks. "Always with your hands over your...thing. It looks like you're playing with yourself. Really! It does. And you are always slumped over—like you are going to take a nap, or something—you are!" ("You ah" in her Bostonian accent.) "How come you can't sit up straight? Is it against your religion or something? And you pick your nose too. You do so! I watch you. It is a disgusting habit!"

She pulls a brush through her thick auburn-colored hair. She's wearing skin-tight blue jeans, a red pullover shirt, and black knee-high boots. Those boots have always meant trouble for me. She glances into the mirror on the wall.

"You would be a classy guy if you did not pick your nose. You would! You would, Boo-bah. If you stopped with the nose and wore some decent clothes, instead of jackets with big holes in the elbows, you would be a classy guy."

I am, for reasons known only to her, "Boo-bah." She is "Dumby" (because, in a way, she is). She puts the brush down on the coffee table and walks to the kitchen, tiny and white-walled. She has a small waist but a broad box-shaped behind. I hear her take the jug from under the kitchen sink and pour herself a drink.

"You know what I think your problem is," she says from the kitchen. "You were left alone too long as a baby. They left you alone way too much. Really, I do! That is why you are so... retarded (re-tadh-did). Really!"

She returns with her drink.

"I am retarded?"

"Yes, you are retarded. Are you kidding?" She smiles brightly. Her face lit by the small shining white teeth. "What do you think you are, normal? Brother! (Bruth-er!) Let me clue you in Boo-bah. Normal people do not pee in bottles and glasses. Normal people use the toilet. What is it with you and peeing in the bottles and glasses? Have you always done that? I don't get it. Is it some kind of childhood rebellion thing? Or what?"

She takes a gulp of her drink. Her cheeks are flushed. "You really ought to see somebody," she says. "I am serious. I think you got, like, a couple of bats in the belfry."

"And you are 'normal'? Is that it?"

"Compared to you? Yes!" She laughs as she swishes wine around in her glass. Takes a big gulp. Seats herself in the only other chair in the room. Looks around the apartment, at the 12-inch black & white TV, with coat-hanger stuck into it, and at the "couch," a long-sized padded lawn-chair deal..."Ain't life a pisser (piss-ah)?" she remarks.

The telephone rings in its cradle. Dumby picks up the receiver. "Hello? Oh, hi Jimmy," she says pleasantly. "Yes, he is right here (heah)." She cups a hand over the receiver. "It is your 'friend,'" she says sarcastically.

"Good news, Kelly," Jimmy Mahoney says in his loud barking voice. A voice that crawls through the telephone and grabs me by the throat. "Trudy says sh sh sh sh might publish a couple of your poems as broadsides."

"O yeah? Really?"

"Yeah, really! Doesn't that make you happy?"

"Yea, I'm happy. I will be happier when I see them."

"You don't think she will do it?"

"I don't know. Will she?"

"Sh sh sh why am I stuttering again?" he asks rhetorically. "She says so...My book will be in print this week. Big Al Dugan came through with a blurb for the book jacket. He compares me to Williams. William Carlos Williams. You know who he is, right?"

"Yes, I do. Hey, that is good company, man."

"I never understood Williams."

"No ideas but in things."

"What does that mean?"

"Means no abstraction, I think. Ideas are already in things. The things therefore are important, not the ideas."

"Humm...You are coming to my book party Friday night, right? Two car loads of people are coming in from Wyoming and a bunch of people are flying in from Boston. Three of my four brothers will be there. Plus my uncle will be there—the gangster—remember I told you about him? Coming down from Chicago. I told him the book is dedicated to him. For his shot in life."

"For his shots in life, you mean."

"Don't be a wise-ass, Kelly."

Dumby is staring straight ahead, into space.

"Yes, I will be there."

"Catch you on the rebound," Mahoney says before he hangs up.

"Mahoney says Trudy might publish some of my poems as broadsides."

Dumby's brown eyes turn my way. "Might?"

"Yea."

"Why would Trudy publish your poems?"

"Why? Um...because she is a publisher? Because she likes poetry?"

"Not enough, Boo-bah!"

"Well, why is she publishing Mahoney's book?"

"Why?" Dumby looks amused. "God (Gad), do I have to explain everything to you?"

"You think that–"

"Of course."

I thought of Trudy. Thin and white-skinned with a plain somewhat mousy dough-face; when I first met her she reminded me of a plucked chicken. "I don't think so," I said.

"Wake-up, Boo-bah!" Dumby polished off her drink. "The world is not what you think it is!

2.

I do not really like cocktail parties. Standing with a drink in my hand and making chit-chat. I don't really like talking all that much, and generally don't, unless forced to (like ordering at a restaurant).

What happens at these parties is I become uncomfortable and have to drink more to feel comfortable again, and when the drinks are not enough to do the trick, to make me the least bit comfortable, I turn to drugs, which leads to an increasingly faster rotation of drink/talk/drug/talk until, at some point, I am moving non-stop, circling from bar to living room to bathroom to front porch to god knows where else until I am so tired I have to sit or lie down somewhere (like under the table).

Mahoney's party was in the fancy home of a wealthy liberal couple, patrons of the arts, and supporters of Bird Wing

Press, the publishing business run by Trudy and her husband. In attendance were poets published by Bird Wing, many in Bird Wing's prestigious "Flying Poetry Series" of books. There were also ex-classmates of Mahoney's from the University; oil workers from Wyoming wearing cowboy hats and boots (Mahoney had once worked in the "patch"); neighbors of Mahoney's from his housing subdivision; people Mahoney had met on the street and in bars...Janitors, lawyers, factory workers, dope dealers, ex-cons...Security personnel from the University (Mahoney had once worked as security guard), university professors, homosexuals, lesbians, a girl dressed in black and wearing a studded dog collar...transsexuals...multi-sexuals...

The Uncle had a face like a piece of flint. He sat on a couch in the living room and was brought drinks by Mahoney who fawned over him. The Uncle did not engage in chit-chat. I did not like the way the guy looked at me: like I amused him somehow; like he was marking me maybe for some job or other, or a hit, on me or by me...

"Kelly!" Mahoney's barking brass voice cut through the smooth jazz playing on the stereo, and the babble of voices, like a billy-club-swinging cop through hippies. "How often do we get together, anyway?" he asked, throwing an arm around my shoulder.

"Maybe too often."

"Sounds like a personal problem, Kelly." Mahoney took a slug of beer from a bottle held loosely between his middle and index fingers. "Come with me, I want you to meet someone," he said, walking me out the front door of the house and onto a deck where people stood in scattered groups.

"This is Ed Lanson." Mahoney pointed to a bearded slope-shouldered man standing alone, a joint pinched between his thump and forefinger.

"Big Ed!" Mahoney barked. He squeezed the short man's bicep. "How are you doing, Pumpkin?"

Big Ed exhaled a stream of pot smoke.

"Ed is a poet. He won the Milton Hopgood Award at the University—same as me."

"An exclusive bunch," Ed said. "You, me, Donald Hall, Robert Bly..."

"And about ten-thousand others, right?" Mahoney said, reaching for the joint. "How is Hall, by the way?"

"Good, as far as I know."

"Ed was drafted by the Detroit Tigers out of High School," Mahoney said.

I heard a loud squeal and turned to see the source. A squeal of joy and mischievousness in equal measures.

Mahoney's blonde haired wife ran up the front steps, her low-cut heeled shoes slapping the rungs. She held the hem of her thigh-length dress in both hands; as she reached the top step she pulled the dress up to her chest and cackled delight- edly. She rotated on her feet and shook her backside; she wore black nylons and underwear.

"Bevy!" Mahoney cautioned. "Don't do that!" He rushed to her side and pulled the dress down then straightened the material like smoothing a curtain. Bev's eyes glittered like gem stones in her handsome face. She stood like an obedient child as Mahoney fixed her dress. "I want a drink!" she screeched.

Bev ran into the house. Mahoney followed.

Ed stared after Bev. "Holy shit," he said, laughing.

Ed passed me the joint. "I never actually played for the Tigers," he said. "I was not that good."

I sucked the smoke in from the evil weed.

"Where do you know Mahoney from?" Ed asked. "Did you go to the University?"

"No. He was my roommate at Frothington State University in Massachusetts."

"Oh. You are 'Kelly'—Mahoney tells stories about you."

"Mahoney tells stories about everybody."

Ed chuckled.

My throat felt dry. I told Ed that I would catch him on the rebound and I floated back into the party. Looked at Dumby being nice to a guy from Nigeria with coal-black skin, his ivory teeth flashing on and off like a light bulb. Bev leaned over the Uncle sitting like a King on the couch. Bev's milk-bottle-shaped tits hung in front of the guy's face. The woman of the liberal couple stood to one side of the Uncle, holding the Uncle's gun, a .38 revolver, in her hands and turning it side-to-side as if looking for an inscription or maybe a price tag; she wore granny glasses and a long svelte expensive hippy dress...One of the cowboys ya-hooed and lifted Terry, a well-known flamer, over his, the cowboy's, shoulder, and held him there like a log. Terry squealed and demanded to be put down, volubly protesting, his face flushed and happy-looking. One of the cowboys made a joke I caught only part of: something about "packing the fudge." Raucous laughter erupted.

"Hello Boo-bah," Dumby said. She wore a flounced dress with modest neckline and puffed sleeves. A cute outfit—for a 7th grade girl going to her Spring Fling. "Your eyes look awful," she said.

"Thanks. That gives me confidence to mingle."

"Mingle? You? That'll be the day." A little smile passed over her cute face; lashes fluttering above doe-eyes.

"Yea, me." I walked across the carpet and stood by Jimmy Steinman, who was watching Bev. Steinman had bushy hair and a hooked nose; his eyes looked like two piss holes in a snowbank. He handed me a lit joint. "Kelly!" he barked (in imitation of barking Mahoney). "How you liking the party?" He elbowed me. "Look at Bev!"

Bev was dancing with some weight-lifting geek with twenty-two inch biceps. She was doing a wild can-can, lifting her dress up around her waist and throwing her legs out.

I saw Mahoney standing in a doorway across the room, watching. His face gloomy.

I heard glass shatter and a flurry of commotion in a distant living room corner. The woman of the liberal couple rushed to the corner (after handing the pistol back to the Uncle).

"Fucking Mahoney," Steinman remarked, "getting published." Seinman smiled, eyes narrowed to slits.

I glanced at Trudy, standing in a group outside of the kitchen door. A group of admirers probably, sucking her unattractive ass. I imagined her laying on her back with her legs spread. Would she publish my poetry? Because...she liked what I wrote? That was doubtful, I thought. My poems were shit, I told myself. I was dreaming to think anyone would publish them. Try prose, I thought. And maybe if I worked hard enough, long enough...Who knows? I could become another... Chandler Brossard. Maybe.

Demented

The tiny woman, barely five feet tall, stood in the kitchen doorway, her suitcases piled like building blocks beside her. A black overcoat hung to her knees and a black hat with uplifted black veil sat like an overturned bowl on her snow-white hair. Black shoes, black gloves, and a black pocketbook, hung from the crook of her arm, completed her ensemble.

The old lady frowned, mouth down-turned like a horseshoe, at the approach of a squat square-shouldered woman whose low-cut sensible loafers trod lightly along the carpeted kitchen floor. The dark-haired dark-eyed woman's chocolate brown dress had a flapping white collar; her stout body filled the aisle between kitchen wall and table.

"Where did you say we were going?" the old woman asked, peevishly, eyes staring behind lenses of black, bat-wing-shaped glasses.

"Ma, I told you a hundred times," the stout woman scolded in her loud-voice. "You are going to live with Albert!"

The old woman's face assumed the obtuse blankness of a mask. She glanced at a man who bustled into the kitchen from the adjoining room. "Who is that?" she asked the daughter, indicating by a nod the short vigorous bald-headed man.

"For Pete's sake," the daughter said, exchanging an un-happy look with the man. "That is Bill, my husband," the daughter said in her booming voice. "We have been married for thirty-nine years," she added, raising her eyes to the ceiling in a comical gesture. The old woman stared at Bill. Bill smiled with a pained expression; he looked down at the red and white checkered place mats on the table top.

"Take these bags out to the car," the daughter ordered. "We have to get moving if we are going to catch our flight."

"Calm down, for cryin' out loud," Bill said gruffly, "we have time."

"I can't calm down," the daughter said. She walked past Bill and into the modest-sized dining room of the ranch-style house. Walking around a table, she straightened a chair and picked up a NATIONAL GEOGRAPHIC. The magazine cover pictured a stalking lioness. Dropping the magazine into a rack, she pulled a tissue from her dress pocket, wiped her eyes, and returned to the kitchen.

"Are you ready, Ma?" she asked.

"Ready as I will ever be."

The daughter steered her mother out of the house and to the car, an older model Cadillac.

During the ride across town the old woman asked where they were going. The daughter said they were going to Albert's house.

"Who is Albert?" the old lady asked.

The daughter exchanged an unhappy look with Bill, riding in the back seat. "Albert is your son," the daughter enunciated clearly. "Your youngest son. He is married to Betty. They have one child: a boy named Timmy."

"Oh no," the old woman interjected heatedly. "Albert never married. He wasn't the kind for girls."

The daughter side-glanced her mother. The old lady had an aged and finely wrinkled spider-webbed face, a face that had once been severe but had become, over the last year —so it seemed to the daughter—oddly child-like. The daughter shifted her gaze to a low stone wall hugging a finely trimmed grassy hillside. A line of white gravestones stood shoulder to shoulder on the face of the hill. Soon her mother would be off her hands, the daughter thought. What a nightmare the last few months had been! The old lady had gone off her rocker, not knowing if she were getting out of bed to start a new day or getting ready to go to sleep; forgetting to dress herself; asking the same questions over and over; compulsively cleaning; obsessing on trivial matters; losing track of what she was doing from one minute to the next. The lucid intervals—there were still a few—becoming ever fewer...Let Albert have his turn at it, the daughter told herself. Albert was younger than she or Bill and Betty would be more help to Albert than Bill, who had medical problems, was to her. Plus Albert and Betty had the boy who could lift and do other things, as needed.

The daughter pulled the car up onto an asphalt plateau beside a tiny wooden box-shaped house at the base of a hilly street lined by tiny box-shaped houses.

Sliding out of the car, the daughter walked up to the back door of the house, which was painted an unearthly blue, shockingly bold; a color rarely encountered in nature, outside of the jungle. The daughter knocked. Her sister-in-law's long angular horse-face appeared in the window, an unhealthy-looking smile plastered on the face. The daughter smiled in return, waiting. When the door did not open immediately, the daughter thought it odd. Betty had, apparently, gone away without opening the door. The daughter's brother's face appeared in the window. Albert's head cannon-ball shaped, slack skin wizened and grayish-tinged, neck creased like a walnut shell. "Well," the daughter thought, feeling foolish and perplexed, "would they open or not?"

The door jarred open with a scrape and bang. "Hello Albert," the daughter said crisply.

"Hi," Albert said, curtly, waving the daughter in.

"Hello, Edna," Betty said, perched on the edge of a cushioned chair in the corner of a small square living room, and still wearing, the daughter noted, the unhealthy-looking smile. "Have a seat." Betty motioned to a chair.

"You want coffee, Edna?" Albert asked as he walked into a kitchen adjacent the living room.

"No thanks," Edna called, standing. "I have got Ma out in the car. Bill and I have to get going if we are to catch out flight." Edna shouted. "Bill has to be early," she said to Betty, "if we are not an hour early he thinks we are going to miss the plane. So, for an hour, we get to sit around and do nothing." Edna chuckled as she glanced at Albert's bowling trophies on top of a TV set and a picture on the wall above the trophies, a seashore scene done in oil and painted, Edna knew, in forty-five seconds by the "world's fastest painter," some guy named Kats. Albert had bragged about the picture after he and Betty had returned from their vacation in Atlantic City. Edna considered what the guy might have done with a few more seconds; still, for forty bucks, or whatever they paid for the thing...Why didn't Betty wipe that goddamn smile off of her face, Edna wondered. She felt like running across the room and slapping the woman.

"You sure you don't want coffee?" Albert asked from the kitchen doorway. A short round-shouldered man with thick bowling-pin shaped forearms, he leaned against the door jamb stirring his coffee.

"No, I don't have time," Edna replied, a bit peeved over the casual way Albert stirred his coffee as well as the tone of his voice. "Like I say, I have Ma in the car," she said, apologetically. "What would you like me to do with her?" Edna smiled. "Where are you going to put her?" She looked past Albert into the kitchen as if it were a possibility.

Albert glanced at Betty. Edna suddenly straightened her shoulders, raising her chin as if she were, once again, standing before an unruly class of Junior High School students in need of being subdued.

"We can't take her," Albert said, all casualness gone from his tone of voice.

"OH YES YOU CAN!" Edna bellowed. "You CAN and you WILL take her!"

"We do not have the room, Edna," Betty argued, sitting rigidly, the smile finally gone. "After Albert's surgery and with his dialysis and with MY mother not feeling well, we just cannot do it!"

"You already agreed, Albert!" Edna said, fighting to keep from shrieking at the peanut-headed little bastard. "It is too late now! There is nowhere else for her to go! NOWHERE!"

"Albert did not know, when he agreed, how sick his surgery was going to make him, Edna." Betty said in a tone of voice that sounded, to Edna, churlish. Edna shot Betty a dirty look. Did Betty think she was talking to a child, Edna wondered. Albert was damn will aware of what he had agreed to!

"You are going to have to take her with you," Albert piped from the doorway.

"Are you CRAZY? We can't take her with us!" Edna roared.

Albert looked to Betty. Betty returned a cow-eyed gaze. Albert had known Edna would put up a fight, but had failed to consider the tone or vehemence of Edna's voice in the confines of the small house. "Well," he said, "how about Anne! Bring her to Anne's house!"

"Anne has five kids," Edna barked. "She is not going to Anne's! She is coming here, Albert, just as you agreed! HERE and NOWHERE else!"

Edna glanced irritably to the doorway on her left, in which stood Timmy, the teenage son, a thin shifty-eyed boy with a shock of hair like a rooster's comb. She felt a sudden surge of hatred for the boy. "I am going to get her," she announced, "and I am going to bring her things in, and THAT is FINAL." She stalked to the door and yanked it open.

From the car, the old woman watched Edna approach. Edna pulled the car door open. "Come'on Ma," she said, repressing an urge to yank the old woman out of the car. "It is time to go!"

The old woman gave Edna a trusting look and turned to debouch.

"Get the bags," Edna hissed at Bill. Bill gave Edna a searching look, eyes narrowed to slits behind his coke-bottle thick glasses.

"They won't take her," Edna snarled.

"WHAT?"

"You heard me." Edna grasped her mother's arm. "They won't take her: But she is going in anyway!" Edna steered her mother toward the door of the house.

"This is crazy!" Bill shouted, jumping from the car.

Edna reached the stoop of the doorway, her mother in tow. Edna's hands were sweat-slicked; a headache throbbed in the middle of her skull.

The door was locked.

Edna rapped on the window pane. Rapped a second time, then a third.

"Must be nobody home," the old woman said helpfully.

Edna sighed and cast a glance upward as if seeking help in the pale blue autumn sky. Bill stood in the driveway looking at the door; he carried six bags.

"Sit down, Ma," Edna said in a stern no-nonsense voice, indicating by a look, the stoop.

The old lady regarded the stone slab. Hesitantly, she allowed Edna to lower her to the step. The old lady pulled the hem of her topcoat over her knees and folded her hands in her lap. "I hope Dad comes home soon," she said, looking down the drive. "Sometimes he has to work late."

"Put those bags down," Edna commanded.

"Where?" Bill asked.

"ANYWHERE!" Edna bellowed. She pointed to the leafy grass beside the stoop: "THERE!"

Bill set the bags down like a harried baggage handler.

Edna jogged to the car, pulled the driver's side door open and squeezed into the front seat. Bill looked in befuddlement from his mother-in-law to the car.

"Get in!" Edna screeched.

Bill walked slowly to the car, looking over his shoulder at the old lady. He climbed into the front seat.

The old woman waved at the car, a bright smile crossing her face.

"Bub-bye," she mouthed.

The car tires barked as the car backed out of the drive. Edna stared fiercely at the side of the unearthly blue house. Her headache throbbed above her right eye. Soon, she would be lying on the beach in Florida, she thought; and then she would forget everything.

6 Lean Pork Chops

He knew his wife was cheating on him. Knew it. Knew it knew it knew it. Knew it like he knew the time of day (2:23 PM). Knew it like he knew his name: Raymond P. Peck, "Raymond" not "Ray." Don't call me Ray; it is Raymond to you. Pal.

Concerning his name, Raymond P. Peck had straightened out plenty of wise-asses down at the plant where he worked, and elsewhere. Told them to their faces: "Raymond" not "Ray." Don't like it? Then "Mister Peck" would do. For you. Punk.

He knew that because of the straightening the punks did not like him. Knew it like he knew his wife was stepping out. Knew it like he knew the punks at the plant called him "Peckerhead" and "Pecker." He'd heard them use the names, the other machine operators, the ones whose lockers were in the first aisle, opposite his. The guys in his aisle did not use the names—not within his hearing. They would not dare, he knew, to use the names to his face. They knew, and he knew they knew, he kept a gun in his locker (Smith & Wesson .38 cal.), double locked by two stainless steel combination locks. They knew he'd use it, too. He knew they knew. Knew they knew they knew. Knew it for a fact. Knew it like he knew his daughter's age. Eighteen. Sally Peck, a cute little package. As prettily packaged as his holstered revolver. So pretty, people gawked at her. Where did Sally get her looks, Raymond often wondered. The wife was no beauty, never had been, and although Sally has his brains—she was at the State University—she did not resemble him (some people thought so, but he knew different; he knew better). The mystery of Sally's beauty led Raymond to occasionally ponder uncomfortable-type thoughts, thoughts that ate at his brain like his ulcer at his stomach.

He pitched his cigarette butt out the pickup truck window. The smoldering butt bounced once in the dirt and came to rest beside a pile-up of previously discarded butts. The butts made a little graveyard of tiny toppled grave stones. The dashboard clock read 2:33 PM. He knew he'd have to drive like a bat out of hell to make it to work on time. Knew he could do it. Knew it like he knew that sooner or later he'd catch the guy who was putting the boots to Irma (or guys—he would not put it past her to have more than one).

A brown box-shaped UPS truck rolled to a stop in front of the Knowlton residence, Laila & Buck, 13 Prospect Street. Raymond stared at the driver. Was the driver making it with Irma, Raymond wondered. Was Buck Knowlton? Raymond watched the driver walk to the Knowlton's front door. A tall prick with a swagger to his walk, a slight strut like a wary rooster. Watching for the fox, Raymond thought.

The driver returned to the truck. Raymond ground his back teeth; the grinding like the sound a glacier makes moving forward. The truck lurched ahead, growling like a beast. As it approached 15 Prospect Street, home of Mr. & Mrs. Raymond P. Peck, the driver turned his head toward the facade of the squat, gray ranch-style house. The driver's lingering glance was like a kiss bestowed upon the lips of Irma Peck. The duration of the glance, coupled with an obvious hint of possessive scrutiny the glance contained, confirmed all Raymond's thoughts about the driver. No doubt Irma was signaling from the house, and that was why, on this occasion, the driver did not stop, go into the house, and put it to her. (She guessed, or knew, that Raymond was watching.) A curtain pulled or left open. A shade up or down. A light on or off. Easy. Easy and workable. Simple but expedient.

Raymond stared at the driver as the truck bucked past, heading north. The driver did not look at Raymond, parked alongside a billboard, advertising SLICK'S WORRY FREE CONDOMS. Buy 'em by the box!!

Raymond trailed the truck up onto the plateau of Upper Prospect Street. Stopping beneath the overhanging branches of a roadside oak, Raymond slumped, eye-level with the steering wheel. The driver plodded across a lawn, moving through bright late afternoon sunshine, arms cradling a stack of packages. A sturdily-built youth, curly-haired with blunt features. The kind of guy, Raymond thought, women would go for. The macho-type. Plus the uniform thing. An image of the driver stuffing his MEMBRUM VIRILE into Irma flashed through Raymond's mind like an excised cut of a porno film. A gust of wind ripped through the oak, and tree branches creaked like rusty hinges of a swinging door. The uniformed whore-master jumped into the brown truck. The wind hissed through the leaves.

"Shut the fuck up," Raymond said.

He slammed his truck into gear and swung the vehicle across the road in a screaming U-ey. 3:10 PM. He drove onto the exit ramp to I-69. To be late for work was unthinkable; he had not been late in twenty-two years on the job. He drove a hundred miles an hour, passing every prick and cunt on the road. He was a bat out of hell.

Ten minutes into the second shift at Combustible Tech-tonics Inc., Ball Bearing Manufacturer, the plant foreman joked to an operator that Raymond must be dead, or else in the nut house. The operator guessed the nut house.

Raymond punched-in thirteen minutes late. He ran from the time clock as if from a fire. His brown low-cut Hush Puppy's slapped the cement floor of the long gray corridor. Like a halfback running downfield, he navigated through a maze of machinery. Sweat rings the size of softballs stained his button-down short sleeve shirt at the arm pits. His scrawny chest heaved. He moved down the aisle in a controlled frenzy, putting his machines into motion. Sixteen machines, eight each side of the aisle, each shaped like an outboard motor, only motor's upsidedown and capped by a spinning bicycle tire-sized wheel.

The machines wailed, screeched like gravelly-voiced babies, adding their complaints to the roar of the shop, pungent with the odor of oil and carbon and warmed to a mephitic toastiness.

Raymond plucked a clip-boarded stat-sheet from a steel guard rail; glanced at the stat-sheet like a man looking at a parking ticket, let go of the clip-board, punched a button on the rail. He waited for the bicycle tire-sized wheel to stop. He unclamped the top half of the wheel. Peering down at the two dozen silver ball bearings lying in the runnel of the bottom half of the hollowed wheel, he picked out two balls. The warm, slickly oiled bearings were like a pair of nuts. Like his, he thought; like any mans. He imagined the nuts in a sack of soft material. Weighed the sack in his hand. Heard the sack whap whap whap into Mrs. Irma Peck's crotch.

He flung the bearings to the floor; the ball's bounced off the concrete and into a pan of oil beneath the machine. The black glossy pool of oil stirred like the rippling skin of a waking panther.

Who was banging her? Besides the UPS guy and the grocer? (He knew all about the grocer.) The butcher? The baker? The mailman? Salesman? TV-repairman?

Out of the gnashing steel mayhemic uproar a voice came into Raymond's head. The voice of either God or the Devil. Raymond turned and gazed into the unhappy face of the shop foreman.

The foreman's mouth opened and closed in paroxysms of speech. Raymond studied the face, viewing each feature separately, merging the features into a single image. Like focusing a camera lens. The foreman's words flew like twittering birds past Raymond's head. He did not catch even one. He wondered if the foreman, Roger Gizzum, was screwing Irma; wondered how many of the guys in the plant she was putting-out for? Raymond watched the foreman backing away, becoming smaller, becoming a blur. The ball-grinding machines grunted like animals rutting. Uncontrolled orgiastic yelping. Ecstatic moans. Feverish crescendo of climactic cries. Screwing their brains out. Irma spreadeagled in the center of the fuck-fest, squirming, moaning...Snickering gargoyle faces peered from heads raised above machines. Leering faces with mocking grins, watching Irma...

Raymond came-to in the locker room, alone, standing upright before his locker. How he had arrived there he did not know. He opened his locker, reached and took his gun from its holster, plugged the gun into the waistband of his polyester pants.

Seventeen minutes later he was home.

Fading sunshine dappled the drive, front lawn, and house. He stepped from the truck, swung the door shut. Birds fed noiselessly at the feeder outside the kitchen window. Insects hovered silently in the humid air. He could not hear the sound of his footsteps on the walkway as he approached the front door. He felt as if he were moving underwater. Felt as if the act of walking was foreign to him, something he was repeating by rote. Everything suddenly seemed unreal, as if he were inside of a waking dream. Was he real, he wondered, or part of the dream? He felt the weight of the gun tugging at his waistband. The gun was real.

Holding onto the butt of the gun, Raymond pushed open the front door and entered the house. The living room was dark as a cave. Light from a small window lit a path for Raymond through the room. A path like a trail through woods.

The hallway leading to the back bedroom was tunnel-like in its darkness. The bedroom door at the end of the hall was illuminated in white-light. The light hurt Raymond's eyes; he stared at the carpet as he walked. A doorway on his right, the door to Sally's bedroom, was filled with shadow. The shadow stepped into the hall across Raymond's path and disappeared into the gloom ahead.

Raymond stood in the back bedroom door: "So! Where is he?"

Irma Peck frowned at the sock held in her hand. "Where is who?" she said, distractedly, drawing a threaded-needle through the sock.

"The guy you have been fucking!"

Irma swiveled her head; her frozen beauty-parlor hairdo shivered. Her dark-rimmed eyes, accentuating her look of frazzled fatigue, opened wide.

"DON'T DENY IT!"

Irma's hands dropped into her lap; the lap was covered by a white apron worn over a flower-printed house-dress.

"I have proof!" Raymond dug into his pocket, reached and slapped a scrap of paper down on Irma's sewing desk.

Irma read her handwriting from the scrap. "Please send six lean pork chops and one pound ground beef."

"It is a note," Irma offered, looking up. "To the grocer... For pork chops," she pleaded, voice rising. "For ground beef!"

"PORK CHOPS!" Raymond crowed. "And what else? IT IS CODE!" he screamed, spit flying from his lips. "Code between you and the grocer! You and the truck driver! You and Buck Knowlton! Yes, Buck Knowlton! And you! And Roger Gizzum, and you! And everybody, and YOU!"

"Oh Raymond," Irma cried, blanching. "Raymond, you are crazy!"

Raymond stabbed a finger to his chest. "I'm CRAZY? You were the one thought you could get away with it!"

Raymond pulled the gun from his waistband.

Irma's mouth opened wide. Wide as a dinner plate. Wide as a manhole cover. Wide as a cave entrance. Wide as a canyon. Wide as the sky on a night black as ink.

She fell backwards, flopping like a rag-doll onto the carpeted floor.

The birds outside the bedroom window peeped like a frenzied bird-orchestra.

Raymond tucked his gun away. He knew his wife would never cheat on him again. Knew it like he knew the time of day. 4:19 PM. Time to get cleaned up and go back to work, he thought. Start the day over.

Acknowledgement

The author would like to thank and acknowledge the following publications, in which some of these stories previously appeared: The Puckerbrush Review, Gihon River Review, Alien Buddha Zine, Horror Sleaze & Trash, and 63-Channels.

About the Author

Wayne F. Burke has lived in the central Vermont area for the past 35 years. He is retired, after working ten years as LPN (licensed practical nurse). Previously held jobs include substitute schoolteacher, journalist, illustrator, dishwasher, fry cook, bartender, moving man, security guard, machinist, truck driver, laborer, janitor, sign painter, roughneck, and orange picker. His first full-length poetry collection was published in 2013 when he was fifty-eight years old. He has published seven additional volumes since. TURMOIL & Other Stories is his first published book-length work of fiction...

Critical response to Wayne F. Burke's poetry:

"...original and authentic. Poetry as funny and as tragic as could ever be imagined. Poems that come from a life-time of real experience in the REAL world, and straight from the heart." Howard Frank Mosher, author, A STRANGER IN THE KINGDOM, winner, New England Book Award.

Wayne F. Burke was born in a small manufacturing town in the remote northeast corner of Massachusetts in 1954; the year of hurricane Edna, which reached as far inland as Berkshire County in western Massachusetts. His father, Ed, had been a sergeant in the Marine Corp before becoming manager of a Mobil Flying-A Gas Station; his mother, Claire Burke nee Kelly, had worked in a textile mill before becoming a full-time housewife. Both his parents died young. His mother at twenty-eight, at which time his father moved him and his three siblings to the home of the paternal grandparents. His father at thirty-two. His grandparents and an uncle raised him and his siblings. His grandfather owned and operated BURKE'S INN, a generational business begun previous to the First World War. During his youth, he was preoccupied with sports and dreamed of becoming a major league baseball player. From Little League through American Legion ball, when his career ended, he was, perennially, an All-Star player. As a high school football player, he was an All-Class A selection during his senior year, and at the University of Massachusetts, Amherst, he was a non-scholarship member of the freshman football team. He was also a history major with vague ideas of becoming either coach, teacher, or lawyer. After encouragement from a professor of rhetoric at the University (earlier encouragement from a High School English teacher), he turned to writing and began first attempts to publish, sending essays and stories to popular magazines of the day (but to no avail). He dropped out of the University after two semesters, worked for six months then returned to college, attending the 2nd institute of higher learning, of the four he eventually attended. As a student at Goddard College, in Vermont, he completed a chapbook of poems. After graduating from Goddard, he continued to write, but sporadically. In the late 1980's he published a smattering of prose fiction, poetry, book reviews and essays, and continued through the 90's to publish irregularly. After the turn of the century his poetry began to be widely published, primarily in Indie publications, online and in print. Besides his eight published poetry collections to date, he has completed a novel, titled THE AGE OF MAMMALS, and is currently seeking the book's publication.

In 2013 he published WORDS THAT BURN the first of his six published full-length poetry collections (five with Bareback Press, one with Alien Buddha Press). Besides the poetry collections, he has published, to date, two poetry chapbooks (Epic Rites Press) and two works of literary criticism. A 7th poetry collection, as well as a novel, titled A NARROW VALLEY, are currently circulating among publishers. Meanwhile, his poetry and prose continues to appear in a wide variety of publications, both online and in print.

—

Made in the USA
Monee, IL
24 November 2020